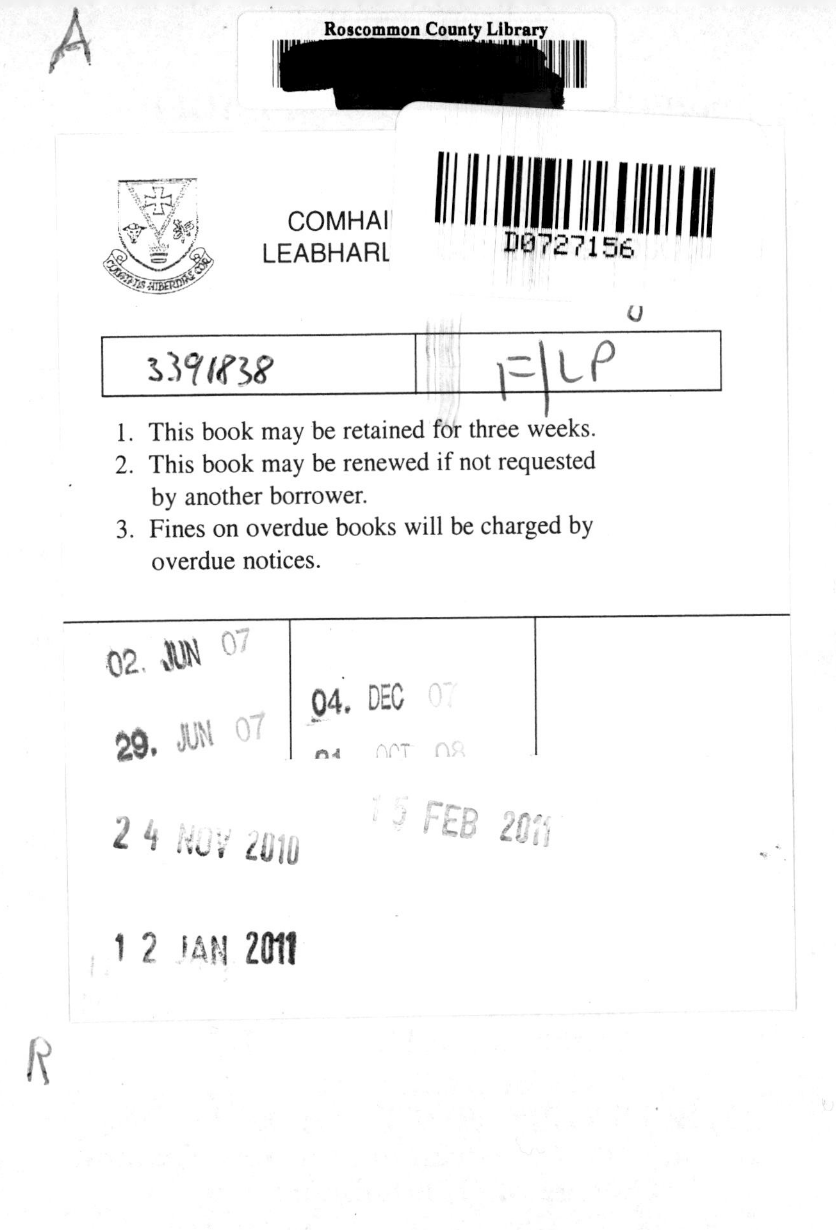

SPECIAL MESSAGE TO READERS

This book is published under the auspices of

THE ULVERSCROFT FOUNDATION

(registered charity No. 264873 UK)

Established in 1972 to provide funds for research, diagnosis and treatment of eye diseases. Examples of contributions made are: —

A Children's Assessment Unit at Moorfield's Hospital, London.

•

Twin operating theatres at the Western Ophthalmic Hospital, London.

•

A Chair of Ophthalmology at the Royal Australian College of Ophthalmologists.

•

The Ulverscroft Children's Eye Unit at the Great Ormond Street Hospital For Sick Children, London.

You can help further the work of the Foundation by making a donation or leaving a legacy. Every contribution, no matter how small, is received with gratitude. Please write for details to:

THE ULVERSCROFT FOUNDATION,
The Green, Bradgate Road, Anstey,
Leicester LE7 7FU, England.
Telephone: (0116) 236 4325

In Australia write to:

THE ULVERSCROFT FOUNDATION,
c/o The Royal Australian and New Zealand
College of Ophthalmologists,
94-98, Chalmers Street, Surry Hills,
N.S.W. 2010, Australia

THE BLUEBELL WOOD

In spring 1865, Silvia Harvey travels to Dartmoor to enter into an arranged marriage with her cousin Gareth. Arriving at Darkwood, Silvia finds Gareth inattentive. Is he really captivated by the lovely Estelle Benedict? And what of her cousin Jared? While the ghost of Samuel Hunter still rules Darkwood, Silvia ponders the fate of her beloved Grandmother Lizzie, as she strives to lay bare the secrets of the old house and the beautiful bluebell wood.

Books by Rosemary A. Smith in the Linford Romance Library:

THE AMETHYST BROOCH

ROSEMARY A. SMITH

THE BLUEBELL WOOD

Complete and Unabridged

LINFORD
Leicester

First published in Great Britain in 2006

First Linford Edition
published 2007

British Library CIP Data

Smith, Rosemary A.
The bluebell wood.—Large print ed.—
Linford romance library
1. Arranged marriage—Fiction
2. Dartmoor (England)—Fiction
3. Love stories 4. Large type books
I. Title
823.9'2 [F]

ISBN 978–1–84617–608–1

Published by
F. A. Thorpe (Publishing)
Anstey, Leicestershire

Set by Words & Graphics Ltd.
Anstey, Leicestershire
Printed and bound in Great Britain by
T. J. International Ltd., Padstow, Cornwall

This book is printed on acid-free paper

Dedicated with love
to the memory of my friend
Beryl Lord of East Budleigh who
appreciated the written word, and
was a wonderful conversationalist.
You are greatly missed.

With thanks to Shelley Tobin, Curator of Costumes at the Albert Memorial Museum, Exeter, for showing me Mary Tucker's wedding dress (c.1864), and for her valued advice on weddings in Victorian times.

1

The house was quiet on April 23rd 1851, as Lizzie Hunter made her way quietly down the staircase at Darkwood, she stopped at the bottom, although trying to be as quiet as she could, her breathing seemed laboured in the stillness of the hall. She pulled the fur-trimmed green cloak and hood she wore tighter with one hand, clasping the bag she carried with the other.

Before stepping out of the heavy oak door, she looked almost furtively around her, and stopped for some seconds before closing the door as quietly as she could behind her, praying no-one would be walking outside at three o'clock in the afternoon. She knew Samuel would be resting, and Gareth and Jared would be with their governess, Miss Pinkerton, at this time of day. It had all been a question of timing so no-one would see her slip out of the house.

Reaching the bottom of the steps, and keeping as close to the house as possible, she made her way across the path toward the small bridge which led to Darklady's Wood. She stood on the bridge, looking for a couple of minutes at the River Dart gurgling merrily on its way across the moor. The sound of it caused her to have a fleeting doubt as to what she was about to do, for she loved the river and the moor. It was the house she loathed, and Samuel. This thought strengthened her resolve and she crossed the bridge with willing feet, stepping out into the wood beyond.

Walking on through a carpet of blue, for the bluebells abounded here this year, she lifted her skirts and took one last look at the house behind her. She'd escaped and breathed a sigh of relief, her life at Darkwood was finally over.

* * *

An icy March wind blew across the moor penetrating through the iron railings which surrounded the small graveyard. I drew my blue cloak tighter around my shivering body surveying the tombstones of my ancestors. The only relief, a small clump of snowdrops which had pushed their way defiantly through the dank earth.

'Silvia!' my mother's strident voice carried across to me from the waiting carriage. She was petulant at having to leave her comfortable home in Exeter to chaperone me to what she called, 'This godforsaken place', known as Dartmoor and Darkwood, her family home. I looked down at the grey tomb, the words jumping up at me. *Here lies Samuel William Hunter, Master of Darkwood 1795–1864. Rest in Peace.*

A year had passed since I stood on this very spot at my grandfather's burial. I idly wondered, as I had twelve months ago, where my grandmother, Lizzie Hunter, was buried. I'd walked in and out of the small collection of tombs and gravestones and could find no evidence of her final resting place. To me, Lizzie was a beautiful memory.

As a small child I could snuggle up to her fragrant bosom while she read stories to me, her cream-coloured skin and black hair gleaming in the firelight. She had a voice which was soft and coaxing and I loved her, a love that had stayed with me all my twenty-one years, but one day Lizzie had vanished out of my life and visits to Darkwood were never the same again. In fact, after her disappearance, when I was about eight years old, we rarely visited again.

Pulling my cloak ever tighter around me, I recalled again the day of Grandfather's funeral and the reading of his Will in the cold study at Darkwood. No mention was made of my grandmother, the only words imprinted in my memory read out by Mr Simms, the family solicitor, '. . . and to gain their inheritance of Darkwood, my granddaughter, Silvia Harvey, and my grandson, Gareth

Samuel, do marry when Silvia has attained the age of twenty-one years.'

I could still hear the gasps of surprise from my Aunt Rachel and her sister, Hannah. I could see the fleeting look of surprise on my cousin Gareth's face and hear cousin Jared's devil-may-care remark, 'It could be worse brother, at least our cousin Silvia has a pretty face.'

For some reason, Jared had been left nothing except for a home at Darkwood for as long as he wished, why I could not imagine. It seemed my grandfather had reached out to us all from the grave to dominate our lives forever.

'Miss Silvia!' our maid, Pru, brought me back to the present as she puffed her way up to the iron gate holding on to her bonnet, which the wind was determined to dislodge from her mop of ginger hair.

'Miss Silvia, the Mistress is getting quite restless. She will wait no longer and you must be freezing in this chill wind.' Taking a backward glance at the tomb, I followed Pru to the waiting carriage, vowing to come back here on a fine day and continue the search for my grandmother's grave.

As we neared the carriage I stopped to look at the small imposing granite church with its squat tower which was built on a small hill. I could see the narrow path winding its way to the door. It was here at Culmoor Church where in a month's time I would marry Gareth, a man I hardly knew let alone loved. I silently prayed the day would be as miserable as I felt.

'Do get in Silvia, please!' My mother was irritable with the delay. I seated myself opposite her in the carriage. 'What you had to stop here for in this weather I can't imagine.'

'I'm looking for my grandmother's, your mother's, grave,' I replied just as irritably, 'and if no-one, including you, will tell me where she is, I have every intention of finding out.'

'For goodness sake child, I've told you before that's all in the past. What you don't know you can't grieve about.

Pru, pass me that blanket please before I perish, we'll all end up with a chill.'

As Pru tucked the blanket securely around my mother's legs I looked at her and thought how she had changed since my father had died two years ago.

Gone was any trace of the pretty woman she had been, her dark hair was greying and she had gained weight, her only love being food and sitting by the fire sewing. 'And please smile now and then child, and speak to me. You've hardly said a word since we left Exeter, has she Pru?'

'No Mistress, she hasn't,' confirmed Pru winking in my direction. We'd all learned long ago it was best to agree with Hannah Harvey. My mother knocked twice and the carriage moved swiftly along the track which was already hardened by the March winds. We rocked from side to side and I felt physically sick.

Moving to the edge of my seat I could see the moorland stretching away either side of the swaying carriage with bursts of yellow colour from the gorse, and although we travelled some distance I could still see Culmoor Church perched on top of the small hillock with the small village of Culmoor tucked behind it.

'What are you thinking, Silvia? Of your wedding day perhaps?' Mother had asked and answered the question for me.

'Yes Mother I am, but not as the happy event you envisage.' I moved back in my seat and leant my head on the brown leather behind me.

'You ought to be thankful, child, that Gareth wishes to marry you,' was my mother's reply.

'Wishes to!' I repeated my mother's words with some disdain. 'He probably hates the idea as much as I do.'

'As I said to you before, he hasn't said he won't marry you.' Mama's reply was in part true.

'To be honest Mother, I would rather marry cousin Jared, he's amusing. Cousin Gareth is aloof and oh so serious, I've never seen him smile, not even as a child.' Out of the window I could see a Tor looming up before us, we were nearing Darkwood.

'At least Gareth is a gentleman,' I heard my mother say, 'and so was your father. Your grandfather chose husbands for your Aunt Rachel and myself and we've been happy.'

'So it's a tradition,' I exclaimed, 'for the Harvey women to have chosen husbands?'

'Silvia, I will not have you speak to me like that. We are here, mind your manners.' She spoke to me as if I was still her little girl.

The house appeared suddenly close at hand. No railings or gates, but two sweeping cultivated lawns, so in contrast to the stark wildness of the moor. The building itself was long and low, built of granite with a slate roof, ivy covered the right front of the building which relieved the greyness. Already the light from oil lamps and candles were flickering in some of the small leaded windows.

As I looked at the house, which was in some ways so familiar to me, it now seemed different and not so appealing. Did I really wish to marry Gareth for Darkwood? I could hear the River Dart on my left gurgling over the rocks, and could see the small wooden bridge which spanned it and led to Darklady's Wood from which the house had got its name. We had been forbidden as children to go near or enter the wood.

Although I never went near for fear of my grandfather's admonishment, I was sure my cousins, Gareth and Jared, had disobeyed. I recalled them urging me to join them, and when I declined Jared called me, 'goody two shoes.' Sometime later they had returned with tales of ghosts and goblins which only served to make me more afraid. All these thoughts were running through my head as Pru and I assisted my mother from the carriage.

'Do be careful, Silvia!' my mother said sharply as I accidentally trod on her foot. 'Ah, here's Rachel.' As Mother spoke I turned to see my aunt walking towards us, a friendly light spilling from the half-open door behind her which dispersed some of the gloom of the impending evening.

There was no ceremony with Aunt Rachel. Mrs Trigg, the housekeeper, and her underlings would be safely ensconced in the kitchen quarters. As my Aunt Rachel embraced my mother I thought how beautiful she still was, her trim figure encased in a pretty mauve gown with lace at her throat, her jet black hair drawn gently back into a bun with soft ringlets framing her still lovely face. Like us she must be thankful the period of mourning was over and that we could dispense with our black dresses in favour of gayer colours.

'Silvia!' Aunt Rachel quickly embraced me also, 'let us get inside out of this cold wind, you must all be famished after your journey.' As she spoke we all made our way to the welcoming hall. I glanced at the flowerbeds in front of the house and could see coloured crocuses closed up for the night with forget-me-nots dancing around them.

As we stepped into the hall it was good to feel the warmth and I realised how cold I had become since standing in the graveyard. A fire was already burning in the huge hearth.

I noticed nothing had changed. A long highly-polished table stood at the end of the hall and drawn around the fire were brightly-coloured armchairs. I looked up at the ceiling with its oak beams and recalled all the rooms in this old house being the same. A wide uneven staircase covered in green floral carpet beckoned towards the upper floor and I suddenly felt a thrill at being here and knowing that very soon this legacy would be mine.

'Welcome Aunt Hannah and cousin Silvia.' I turned to see Jared walking towards me across the highly-polished floor. He embraced my mother and then taking my hand he raised it to his lips, all the while locking my eyes with his in an unfathomable gaze. There was mockery in that look and also some emotion I couldn't define. Jealousy perhaps that I, a mere female, had inherited Darkwood instead of him.

He was attractive and yet not handsome. His hair neither dark nor fair, he had insipid pale blue eyes that this smile never reached. He was short of stature, being just a little taller than myself but the one thing which stood out about him above all else, he was immaculately dressed and not a hair on his head out of place. I felt a pity for him, why I couldn't say, but quickly removed my icy hand from his grasp.

'You notice, fair lady, that your betrothed is not here to greet you?' I detected a hint of sarcasm in his voice and guessed things were none too friendly between Jared and his brother.

'Please Jared, not now,' my aunt intervened. 'Gareth sends his apologies Silvia, but he has ridden to an outlying farm and will see you at dinner. Now come, Silvia, and I will show you your room. Your mother is in her old room and I have prepared your grandmother's room for you.' So saying my mother heaved herself out of the chair she had sunk into.

Whilst Mother made her way to her old room, I followed Aunt Rachel along the dark corridor, full of excitement at seeing Lizzie's room again. As we stepped in it was just as I had remembered only it seemed smaller. The huge mahogany four-poster bed draped with pink damask curtains took up a good part of the room. A large wardrobe stood in the corner adjacent to the fireplace from which the warmth of the fire already burned.

Under the small window was Grandmother's petite writing desk and a small dressing table and washstand stood by the door. I recognised the china bowl and water jug decorated with pink roses and thought lovingly of my grandmother, while I looked with some longing at the armchair drawn up next to the fire where I had spent many happy hours in her company.

'I can see you are pleased,' Aunt Rachel's voice cut across my thoughts, I'd almost forgotten she was there.

'Why thank you, Aunt Rachel, for giving me this room.'

'I know how much she meant to you, now I must go and see that all is going well with dinner and confirm that Pru is settled. I will see you at dinner at about seven and will have some water and refreshments sent up.'

I went straight across to the writing desk and pulled at the front, but it wouldn't budge. Looking out of the small window above it I observed it was too dark to see anything and would have to wait until morning. Pulling together the pink curtains I looked around again at the room. It had a warm feel like Grandmother and I felt really at home.

I made my way across to the sampler in the wall by the bed. As a child I'd always been fascinated by the picture worked by my grandmother in cross-stitch of a house with four windows and a red front door. As I looked at it now I suddenly felt really close to her and ran my hand gently across the name of the eight-year-old Lizzie Kellaway who had painstakingly stitched it in January 1802.

I looked around at the armchair and wished so much Grandmother was sat there, the longing was almost painful. Opening the wardrobe doors I almost expected to see her clothes still hanging there, clothes of gay colours, but the inside was dark and empty and smelled of mothballs. I ran my hand along the bottom and touched on something which had long been forgotten.

On bringing it out into the light of the oil lamp I could see it was a small lace bag decorated with pink and yellow roses. I pressed it to me and quickly placed it in the dressing table drawer lest someone take it from me, the drawer too was empty, but one thing which remained on top was a small pink perfume bottle. I eagerly picked it up and smelt the rose scent which still lingered.

A slight tap at the door startled me somewhat and almost guiltily I placed the scent bottle back on the dressing table and the door burst open to reveal Gareth. To say I was surprised would have been an understatement and I just stood there looking at him as he stood on the threshold of my room.

Was he taking in my dishevelled appearance? For my long black hair tidy this morning had successfully escaped the pins, my pale blue travelling cloak was grubby from its trailing around the graveyard. To Gareth my violet eyes must have shown their surprise for he smiled, after all I had said earlier he actually smiled.

'It's good to see you cousin Silvia, albeit that it's not just for a family visit.' His voice was deep and precise. I could see he was doing his utmost to be polite. Unlike Jared, my betrothed was handsome, he had the coal black hair of the Hunter family and the good looks to match it. His eyes working over me were almost as black too and he was tall. Whereas Jared was meticulous in dress, Gareth was clothed in a casual air which suited him. He must have come straight to my room as he still wore his black riding cape and boots and while he stood there he tapped his riding crop gently on the palm of his left hand.

I gathered myself together and stood straight and tall quite incensed with him for bursting into my bedroom unannounced. 'I'll thank you not to come to my room again, it's most ungentlemanly and bad mannered on your part,' maddeningly my voice was quavering and my cheeks flushed.

'But we are to be married, Cousin, does this mean you will bar me from your bedroom indefinitely?' It was a challenge and I had no ready answer. I watched him leave and heard the door close quietly behind him and for no apparent reason I burst into tears.

2

My tears subsided, I knew not why they had fallen at all, maybe being back in Lizzie's room again had brought to the fore my emotions at losing her and had brought back sweet memories that I yearned for after all these years. Or could it be that coming face to face with Gareth my betrothed had made me realise to the full what a position I was in.

An arranged marriage by a grandfather whose very presence in a room had filled me with fear and awe. Could I really marry this cousin of mine who was almost a stranger? Or was I missing my friend, Grace Caswell, whose friendship I valued more than anything? I longed for a week to pass so she would join us to be my bridesmaid.

A tap on the door interrupted my thoughts and the door opened to reveal a pretty young maid with blonde curls escaping her mop cap. She gave a small curtsey as she placed a tray laden with thinly-sliced bread and butter, a piece of sponge cake accompanied by a pot of tea with a bone china cup and saucer, on the small table next to the armchair.

'Thank you.' I said, sitting up straighter in the armchair, running my hands gently over the fading pink arms as my grandmother had done. 'What is your name?'

'Dotty, Miss, I'm not to linger, Miss, as I'm needed in the kitchen to help with dinner.' She dropped another curtsey, which I found quite endearing as she headed for the door.

'Oh Miss, almost forgot to say, Douglas is bringing your trunks up.' No sooner had she spoken, there was a tap on the door. Dotty opened it and Douglas, with a young man, carried in one of my trunks and set it behind the door.

'Is it all right there?' he asked in a gruff voice. I nodded in agreement.

'Then me and young Alfred here will go and fetch the other one, Miss, which I'm bound to say is a good deal lighter than the one we've just brought up.'

Dotty was still holding the door open and the three of them went out with Dotty dropping another curtsey before scuttling out and closing the door behind her.

I knew why the trunk Douglas had set to one side of the bed was heavier. It contained my trousseau, which Mother and I had spent all year stitching. How I hated sewing! Books appealed far more to me and I picked up the latest English Woman's Domestic magazine my mother had purchased for me on one of her rare shopping trips. I flicked through the pages with little interest, Dickens and Lord Tennyson being far more to my liking.

On opening the lid of the trunk, I looked at the contents folded in painstakingly neat piles. Nightdresses, petticoats, silk drawers, chemises, corsets, reception dresses, walking dresses, day dresses, shawls, teacloths, towels and tablecloths, everything a new bride would need for the start of married life. When I thought of all the stitches, embroidery and hours of work which had gone into it all, I felt quite tired and slammed the lid shut on it all abruptly, just as Douglas appeared with the second trunk.

Pru arrived, dear Pru she always managed to lighten my mood, in no time she'd arranged all my clothes in the wardrobe and drawers.

'Now what are you thinking of wearing this evening, Miss? I think you should look your best.' As she spoke, her expert hands searched through my many coloured dresses. Almost in triumph she lifted out my favourite violet coloured silk dress, smoothing the skirt and flattening the cream lace collar. 'Well, Miss Silvia?' she asked, as she shook the creation causing the silk to shimmer in the light of the oil lamps.

My lack of interest must have shown. 'Come now Miss, this matches your eyes perfectly and you know it, you will look a picture.' For her sake I smiled.

'All right Pru, you've convinced me, now I must set to getting ready.' I conceded.

'Your future husband will not be able to resist you, Miss, and that's a fact.' As Pru spoke she smiled broadly at me, but this thought dampened my spirits.

'I don't wish to think of him,' I said, far more sharply than I intended, and I laid a hand gently on Pru's arm.

'You may quite like him when you see him, Silvia,' Mother's voice interrupted.

I looked around to see her standing in the doorway, she'd entered so quietly neither Pru nor I had heard her. 'Mother I've seen him, he came to my room not an hour since.' My voice was full of indifference.

'Did he indeed, obviously a man full of spirit and strong intention.' As she spoke, my mother sat herself in Lizzie's chair. 'So child, what do you think of Gareth Hunter?' There was silence for a few seconds. 'Well answer me, child!'

My silence obviously irritated her, but I knew not what to answer. What did I really think of this man who was to be my husband after so brief an encounter? As she sat looking at me her face full of expectancy her mouth slightly open, I knew Mother needed an answer.

'Gareth is a handsome man, this I cannot deny.' The words came out of my mouth slowly and quietly as I continued. 'He is bold and . . . ' I searched for the word, 'and arrogant! There, now you have my answer, please allow me to dress for dinner.' Mother shuffled back in the chair obviously aware that was all I would say.

My crinoline hoop was in place as Pru helped me on with my gown. As I looked in the mirror I acknowledge Pru was right. The violet colour of the gown matched my eyes perfectly. Delicate cream lace adorned the high neckline and the elbow-length puffed sleeves. As I sat at the dressing table Pru deftly fashioned my jet black hair. I was ready to face the Hunters.

Mother had been dozing in the chair, the black skirt of her dress rising and falling with each breath, she suddenly came to and sat up straight.

'Of course, the Reverend George Poulter will be here this evening so Rachel tells me.' She spoke half stifling a yawn, then stood up on her feet, quite precariously as Pru steadied her with a gentle hand.

'Whatever for?' Was my sharp-tongued reply.

'Because dear girl, you and Gareth need to set a date for your wedding.' Mother's tone matched mine.

'We are surely not going to set the date at the dinner table!' I was aghast at the very thought of it and looked at Mother with some anxiety.

'It would appear so, Silvia. Now just you remember your manners especially in front of any strangers we may encounter this evening. I want to feel proud of you, for you look quite lovely this evening.' This was indeed a compliment from Mother and the reply hovering on my lips died as I thanked her if somewhat begrudgingly.

Walking along the corridor our skirts swishing on the carpets beneath our feet, a sudden thought came to mind. My grandmother's portrait had at one time hung at the top of the stairs, I'd not noticed it on our arrival earlier, my steps quickened eager to see the face I so loved.

To my utter disappointment the portrait I longed to see was gone. In its place hung a picture of my grandfather, Samuel. His likeness had been painted standing by a gnarled grey oak, bluebells surrounding his feet and flanked on either side by large spaniel-type brown and white dogs. The portrait had obviously been painted in the latter part of his life for his sparse hair was a steel grey and, as I looked at his face I noted the cruel mouth, half of which curled in a sardonic smile.

'What are you looking so intently at

my father's portrait for?' Mother's breathless voice interrupted my train of thought.

'Because I had hoped to see the picture of your mother and was surprised to see my grandfather instead.' My reply to Mother's questioning was half-hearted, because looking more intently at the wall I could see the faded wallpaper where Lizzie's picture had once hung, obviously being far larger then the one of her husband. I turned to my mother, 'So where has Lizzie's portrait gone?' It was a simple question for me to ask, but I was not to gain a simple answer.

'Goodness child, how would I know. Now let us get down to dinner for we are already late.'

I resolved to locate the missing portrait of my beloved grandmother.

As we entered the drawing-room which was situated at the front of the house, my first thought was that gone were the mellow warm pink colours that Lizzie loved. In their place were bright blues, the curtains and furniture shrieked with the colour and I suddenly felt cold, even though a fire already burned brightly in the old stone hearth.

My second thought was that there appeared to be several people in the room all seemingly unfamiliar except for Aunt Rachel, who amidst hushed silence when we entered steered my mother to a settle by the fire. Before I had chance to look around me a hearty, booming voice uttered my name. 'Silvia!' And I was drawn by two strong arms into a swift embrace. The gentleman put me at arms length and I could see it was Aunt Rachel's husband, my Uncle William, age had not altered him a good deal, he was greyer with bright rosy cheeks, which years on Dartmoor had accorded him. I realised now I was older and how short of stature he was being no taller than myself.

'Why, Uncle William!' I beamed with some pleasure, recalling all the happy times I'd spent with him as a child, playing hide and seek amongst all the nooks and crannies at Darkwood, rolling brightly coloured marbles along the path at the front of the house, me always winning and doing jigsaw puzzles together in the evenings under the dim light of oil lamps.

'You no longer look the tomboy I remember,' he observed. His eyes twinkling. 'What a beautiful young woman you've become. A bright light for eyes as old as mine.'

'Oh come, Uncle,' I bantered, 'You aren't that old, just older.' And we laughed.

'I hear I'm not to give you away at your marriage to my son, Gareth.' At his words my smile vanished. 'You are displeased with this forthcoming union?' my dear uncle queried, his face full of concern.

'Not displeased as such Uncle, more apprehensive.' I replied in a quiet voice, drawing my hands away from his.

'Let it suffice to say for this evening

at least, that I could wish for no more suitable a bride than you for my son.' Uncle William spoke the words quietly also just as we were interrupted by Jared.

'Come now Father, you've spent enough time with our lovely cousin, time for someone else to enjoy the pleasure of her company.' As Jared spoke he steered me to the window opposite the fireplace where a young man and woman were in quiet conversation.

As we approached, the young man looked up, his eyes meeting mine, he was tall with short dark hair the front of which fell appealingly across his forehead.

'Silvia, let me introduce you to the Reverend George Poulter, who will be officiating at your marriage to my brother, Gareth.' As Jared spoke the words I noticed the clerical dress this prepossessing gentleman wore. He offered his hand, 'It is my pleasure to at last meet you, Miss Harvey, and on such a joyous occasion,' Mr Poulter enthused.

The young woman at his side looked on in silence as introductions were made, I fleetingly thought that she looked too young to be his wife for she looked eighteen, and the vicar in his thirties. But I was proved right by his next words.

'Please allow me to introduce my sister, Isabel.' As he spoke he drew the young woman forward. At this point I caught sight of Gareth out of the corner of my eye. I turned to observe him better, he was in earnest conversation with the most beautiful creature I had ever set eyes upon. She was slim and fair, her skin like polished ivory without a blemish, the pale green of her expensive gown matching perfectly with the green of her sparkling eyes.

As I started at the two of them, she suddenly threw back her lovely head and laughed. It was the loveliest laugh I had ever heard, like wind chimes tinkling in a summer breeze, but for some strange reason the sound of it stabbed at my heart like a piece of shattered glass.

3

'Miss Harvey,' the vicar's questioning voice drifted across to me and I turned back to face him.

'Apologies, Vicar, you must think me most rude.' As I spoke I noted that Isabel still hadn't uttered a word. Her pale face showed no expression and she seemed not to notice her surroundings, the yellow dress she wore was garish and did not compliment her pallid colour or her mousy coloured hair.

'On the contrary, Miss Harvey, I can understand you being distracted by your betrothed, especially as he is talking to such a lovely young woman.' His eyes twinkled as he spoke, and while the vicar found this entertaining, I most certainly did not. At this moment Jared offered me a glass of sherry which I took willingly, I would like to have drunk it in one go, but sipped it as decorously as I could.

Looking at Jared, the thought crossed my mind that he would be a far more attentive bridegroom, for Gareth had not even noticed my existence in the room, something I intended to rectify this instant. Swiftly I walked across to him and his beautiful companion.

'Are you going to introduce me to this lovely lady, cousin Gareth, or are you too enamoured to tear yourself away?' My voice trembled as I spoke.

After speaking the words I wished I could have retracted them and I knew that Mother would be furious at my manner. Gareth turned to look at me, an unfathomable expression on his handsome face. I noticed how his black jacket and waistcoat showed off the snow white of his ruffled shirt.

'Cousin Silvia, please let me introduce you to a family friend, Miss Estelle Benedict.' So saying, Gareth clicked his heels together and without so much as an, 'excuse me', left me with this lovely creature whose name matched her beauty, and for an instant I thought of the novel, *Great Expectations*, and idly wondered would Miss Benedict break Gareth's heart or mine.

'Delighted to meet you at last Miss Harvey.' Estelle's voice was as melodic as her laugh. As she spoke she offered a hand which was limp in my grasp. The smile on her face didn't meet her eyes and knew instinctively that she hated me as much as I hated her. Thankfully we were not destined to engage in conversation that evening.

Mrs Trigg arrested our attention by informing us that dinner was ready. She was still a tall thin woman, her greying hair scraped severely back off her face which served to accentuate her large nose. As children we'd laughed about this and my mind flew back to Gareth.

As I looked around I caught sight of him with Aunt Rachel heading for the dining-room. Did he really not care about my existence, for surely, as his betrothed he should have escorted me into dinner. I felt a sense of total frustration at his complete indifference.

As it happened I walked into the dining-room with a silent Isabel, for her brother had escorted the lovely Estelle.

As we entered the dining-room, I noticed straight away the walls were blue as in the drawing-room, although the long dining table was beautifully laid with a white damask tablecloth, silver and crystal goblets, the room felt cold and I shivered involuntarily.

'Silvia, Gareth, please sit at this end of the table.' Uncle William indicated the two seats by him as he was obviously to sit at the head. Aunt Rachel sat next to Gareth and Jared took his seat by me. I found this difficult looking across at my future husband and feeling Jared's nearness throughout the meal. Surprisingly it was Gareth who first mentioned our wedding date.

'When would you like us to marry, cousin?' His words drifted across the table and I realised with some hesitation that Gareth had addressed me.

'I have no thoughts on this.' I replied quietly. 'Sometime next year would suit me, and yourself perhaps?' I asked sweetly.

His reply was unexpected. 'Indeed not, cousin, I had thought of Easter this year.' As he spoke he raised one dark eyebrow.

'But that is only four weeks away!' The alarm in my voice must have shown.

'The sooner the better, cousin. I shall be more than pleased when the deed is done and we can all get on with our lives. Do you agree, Mother?' he turned to Aunt Rachel.

'Why yes, an Easter wedding sounds delightful.' She agreed.

'Indeed it will be.' My mother, who sat next to her sister, responded, 'Not much time to prepare I will admit, but a lovely time of year none-the-less, and I can return to Exeter sooner rather than later.'

I looked at the three of them striving to think of some complication. I then realised that Estelle was in deep conversation, the Reverend Poulter quite oblivious to the discussion at this end of the table. While Isabel sat morosely next to the lovely creature, like a moth next to a colourful butterfly.

Then the thought came to me in a flash, 'But I have no wedding gown,' I said in triumph, looking at them all in eager anticipation. But Mother's words dampened my spirits further.

'No dear, but I'm sure that will be no problem, you have your veil ordered from Honiton, and your head-dress and shoes being made in France, we will just have to inform them that we require an immediate delivery.'

Mother sat back in her chair, white napkin tucked in the neck of her dress, she was obviously tired and well fed.

Aunt Rachel turned her attention to me, 'We have a very good dressmaker in Tavistock, Silvia, who we will visit tomorrow after lunch. There, does that make you feel more at ease, child?'

'Enough of bridal dresses and flowers, there will be time enough to watch my wife sewing in the evenings, let alone talk of it before the marriage.' Gareth spoke firmly and then applied his concentration to the cheese on his plate.

'But Silvia hates sewing or embroidery.' My mother's voice boomed out, causing everyone to look, 'She has more love for her novels and poetry than in normal women's pastimes.'

At this Gareth raised his eyes and looked at me, 'Who is your favourite poet, cousin?' he asked with obvious interest.

'Our Poet Laureate, Alfred Lord Tennyson, our Queen's favourite also.' I replied almost shyly.

Gareth's next words stunned me somewhat. 'The Knights come riding two and two, she hath no loyal Knight and true.'

As he uttered the words, Gareth's dark eyes locked with my violet ones, it was for only a matter of seconds, but in that short space of time I both admired the fact that he quoted from Tennyson's *Lady Of Shalott*, and realised at the same time he was conveying to me the message, 'you have no Knight in me.'

He wiped his beautifully-shaped mouth with his napkin which he then placed on the table. 'So we are agreed, cousin. Easter Saturday, the fifteenth of April it shall be, if this is suitable for you, Reverend?'

'It is indeed, I will call the banns for the next three Sundays. I would like to think you will both attend church.' Reverend Poulter looked at us both.

It was the point that I realised that from now on we would be looked upon as a couple. My heart started racing and I felt my cheeks going hot at the thought, that in four weeks' time I would be sharing my life with a stranger. The men all stood as we ladies retired to the drawing-room, leaving them to their port and masculine conversation.

In the hall, Mother excused herself

and said that she was weary and needed to get to bed, or she wouldn't enjoy our outing to Tavistock on the morrow.

The word, outing, was a most unfortunate term as I looked on it as a chore. We all bade her goodnight and made our way to the drawing-room. Much was said about my forthcoming wedding.

'Have you a bridesmaid, Silvia? For if not, I would be pleased to oblige,' said Estelle at one point in the conversation.

'Thank you for the kind thought, Estelle, but my friend, Grace, is to join us in a week. She will be my bridesmaid.' I replied with little charity.

My aunt sat opposite me by the fire. 'Why have the rooms been decorated in blue Aunt Rachel?' I had to ask.

Did I detect a slight hesitation as she responded, 'Your grandfather wished them to be this colour after . . . ' And her voice trailed away.

'Also,' I interposed. 'Where has Lizzie's portrait gone which hung at the top of the stairs when I was a child?'

‘I really don’t know, but you could try the attic when you have a spare couple of hours,’ Aunt Rachel offered. And I immediately resolved to visit the attic in the morning, for Grandmother’s portrait was more important to me than a wedding gown.

I was tired. The many events of the day were overwhelming, not least my encounters with Gareth Hunter, but I didn’t want to think of him. I excused myself and left the drawing-room.

As I put one foot on the bottom stair of the staircase, my skirt held up at the front with one hand I was stopped by a voice behind me.

‘Cousin Silvia,’ I turned back to see Jared leaning against the dining-room door a goblet of port in one hand. As I looked he raised the glass and quietly said, ‘To you, cousin.’

‘Goodnight, Jared, I am weary and in no mood to play games,’ I said dismissively and turned back to climb the staircase. I was half way up when he gently caught my arm.

'Favour me cousin, for you won't regret it I promise you.' Jared spoke quietly and with some urgency.

'Jared, we cannot talk like this on the staircase, for one thing it is dangerous,' I replied firmly. 'And for another, you must be aware, it is improper given my situation with your brother.'

'Then move up the stairs to the corridor, for I wish to speak with you alone,' he implored.

I did as Jared asked, for nothing could be gained by lingering halfway up the staircase, if for no other reason than that we could be seen. We stepped into the corridor leading to my room when Jared turned me to him.

'You must realise that Gareth will lead you a merry dance. He's only marrying you so he can get his hands on his beloved Darkwood, whereas I hate the very name of this house, and could take you away and give you more attention than my brother ever will.' He paused, 'Please at least say that you will mull it over,' he implored again.

Pulling my arm away from his grasp I realised I felt intimidated and unsure as to how to handle this unexpected situation. I knew that to humour him was the only way of dealing with him, for the moment at least.

'I will agree to think about it, Jared, but now I wish to get to my room. Sleep is what is needed for I cannot think straight without it.'

My words seemed to please him for he made to descend the stairs, stopping briefly to say, 'You must know that Gareth only has eyes for Estelle Benedict.'

I stood there for some seconds and then I heard him bid Gareth goodnight. I quickly realised the two brothers must have passed on the staircase and with some sense of alarm as Gareth appeared, I wondered if he had heard any of our conversation.

My betrothed looked at me, bid me goodnight, then strode in the opposite direction.

Entering my bedroom, I leaned back

against the door, relieved that I was back in Lizzie's room. In the hearth, embers of the fire still glowed brightly and I sank into my grandmother's armchair, a hundred thoughts whirling in my head.

Why had Jared made this declaration and if I accepted, where would he take me? As far as I was aware he had no means of supporting me. I was sorely tempted, but that thought led me to Gareth, could I in time get to know this stranger, and even given time, love him?

Yes I thought, I will accept the challenge, and made a mental note not to find myself alone with cousin Jared, but this I was to learn, was going to be easier said than done.

The door opening startled me, but it was only Pru. 'Come to help you prepare for bed, Miss Silvia. You look done in and that's a fact. A good night's sleep will refresh you so you will be ready to see everything in a new light tomorrow.' Pru chatted on hardly aware that I was quiet and unresponsive.

I climbed into Lizzie's bed, the feather mattress curling around my weary body, I snuggled into the pillows and thought about Grandmother. It was all very strange, no headstone in the graveyard and her portrait removed, for what reason I had yet to find out, but had every intention of scouring the attic in the morning. My last thought as I snuggled under the covers and drifted into sleep was what did cousin Gareth think of me, did I care? And the answer was, yes.

4

The following morning, attired in my powder blue day dress, I sat at the dining table alone. It would appear no-one else ate breakfast and I half expected Jared to appear, but prayed not. This was the day I would explore the attic before our trip to the dressmakers.

Making my way across the hall to find Mrs Trigg to ask if I needed a key to the attic door, I encountered Aunt Rachel.

'Ah Silvia, I was looking for you. Did you sleep well?' Aunt Rachel put a hand over mine as she spoke. Not waiting for an answer she continued, 'There is a change of plan, we are to visit the dressmaker this morning.'

'I was just about to explore the attic,' I said with some sense of disappointment.

'Never mind dear, you can do that on our return. Gareth has to go to Tavistock for some painting oils, so we may as well all go together. Your mother is getting herself ready as we speak, we'll meet in the hall at nine-fifteen.' With these words Aunt Rachel left me to make her way up the stairs, so I thought I'd best do the same.

To think I would be in close proximity to Gareth in the coach caused me some concern. On the other hand maybe it was a chance to draw him closer to me and vanquish the lovely Estelle from his mind.

All duly attired and settled in the coach, we made our way slowly across the moor. The wind had ceased today and the sun shone brightly on the windows of the coach. I felt stifled by the green cloak I wore and untied the ribbon around my neck, almost dislodging my bonnet.

Mother was snoozing in one corner, Aunt Rachel was looking out at the moor in all its glory, greens, browns and yellows were dappled by the sunlight and fluffy white clouds, the whole landscape seemed to stretch into infinity impeded only by intermittent slabs of granite, and I was watching Gareth who sat opposite me.

'What are your thoughts, cousin Gareth?' I bent towards him as I spoke. He looked at me for some moments before replying.

'I am thinking the pale green becomes you and that your bonnet is very pretty.' This was a compliment indeed and I felt my cheeks going hot praying Gareth did not notice my confusion at his words. It was my favourite bonnet, the edge trimmed with pink lace, and the bonnet itself adorned with small pink rosebuds.

I noticed Aunt Rachel glance at us before turning back to the window, a gentle smile on her face, she was obviously pleased at the way the conversation was going.

'Why thank you, cousin,' I responded quietly. 'I understand that not only do you recite poetry, but you paint as well.'

'I only dabble in it from time to time, but it is relaxing and enjoyable, I have a small studio at the top of the house next to the attic.' My thought was that my betrothed was very talkative and forthcoming today, could it be because of the absence of Miss Benedict? He continued, 'Our grandmother painted, did you know she came from Ireland?'

'No I did not, but she had no accent so I had not realised,' I replied with some interest. 'Where did she come from?'

'Killarney in Southern Ireland, it is said that Grandfather fell in love as soon as he set eyes on her, and I suspect she lost her Irish brogue while living so long at Darkwood.'

Having spoken, Gareth looked out of the window, 'We are here,' he said, and as I looked I could see that we were in a small market town with sand-coloured buildings. Everywhere was a hive of activity, people selling their wares and children chasing hoops along the thoroughfare.

The carriage jolted to a halt outside a very imposing double-fronted building with a large bell under the roof. I guessed we were at the dressmaker's and felt quite cheated that the interlude with Gareth had ended so abruptly, but also felt that we had built part of the rapport so needed between us.

Mother opened her eyes, obviously woken by the stopping of the carriage, she looked at Aunt Rachel, a bemused expression on her face.

'We're surely not here already, I'd only just nodded off. No matter, let us hope we achieve what we've come for.' As Mother spoke she wriggled to the edge of her seat and Aunt Rachel helped her to her feet, her mauve dress getting caught under one shoe.

Gareth opened the door and jumped down nimbly offering his hand to help me alight. It was the first time I'd had physical contact with him and was somewhat surprised to find the touch of his hand grasping mine was a pleasant experience.

He helped Mother and Aunt Rachel out also saying, 'This is where I leave you ladies, I will return for you in two hours.'

The three of us stood at the door awaiting an answer to the bell we'd just rung. I was interested in the highly-polished brass plaque to the left of the door inscribed with the words, *Caroline Peacock, Dressmaker*.

After greeting us, we were led into a room on the right by Caroline herself. She was slightly overweight with a rounded figure encased in a ruby coloured dress which suited her blonde wavy hair and rosy cheeks perfectly. As we stepped into the room we were confronted by bales of material in every hue and colour.

'This is all I have in silk, but I'm sure Miss Harvey, that you will find something here to your liking,' Caroline addressed me as she spoke, for my mother and aunt walked in and out of the tables looking at various materials. I was drawn to a dove grey silk and as I smoothed my hand across it Mother's voice came to me.

'Not grey, Silvia, please,' she admonished. 'Here is an ivory silk taffeta far more appropriate.' I walked over to where Mother had indicated.

'But grey matches my mood, Mother.' As I spoke the words, I realised they weren't strictly true now, for part of me was looking forward to a match with Gareth and I decided at that moment to enjoy the preparation for my inevitable union. 'This is indeed quite lovely and will match my lace veil well,' I said, quite astounding Mother as she had, I think, been prepared for a battle.

'You've chosen well, Miss Harvey, and may I suggest that as your veil is lace, your dress should be plain,' Caroline asked me tentatively.

'I do agree, and what style do you recommend?' I asked with some enthusiasm, for if this marriage were to take place, which indeed it would, I wished to look at my most captivating for my bridegroom.

'I think perhaps a long-sleeved neat bodice, separate from the skirt, which should be full at the back to suit your slim figure and height.' As she spoke Caroline was looking me up and down.

'I will bow to your knowledge, Miss Peacock. I am confident you will make me a wedding dress that I will adore.' As I spoke I looked at Mother and could see unshed tears in her eyes. She was very emotional about the whole situation, which I found quite endearing.

Caroline asked us to return in a fortnight for a fitting. As we stepped outside the carriage was waiting as Gareth had promised. We were all silent on our way back to Darkwood, each with our own thoughts, Mother and Aunt Rachel no doubt like me thinking of the forthcoming wedding, even more so as I surveyed Gareth's handsome face, the expression of which was inscrutable and I wondered to myself just what he was thinking.

We arrived back at Darkwood in time for a light lunch. Much to my disappointment, Gareth declined to join us, and after eating I sped upstairs to change. My visit to the attic and Lizzie's portrait being uppermost in my mind.

Aunt Rachel had pointed me in the right direction and there was indeed a key which she had handed to me with the words, 'Don't fall over anything.'

I had to turn left at the top of the stairs, along the corridor Gareth had walked the evening before, and as I passed each door I was left wondering which room was his, but resisted the strong temptation to step through each door with the hope of finding out.

Sure enough, as Aunt Rachel had directed, at the end of the corridor to the right was a narrow plain wooden staircase. I walked up it slowly, lifting my skirts as I went. As I rounded the corner at the top I was confronted by a low door and I inserted the key, and with some anticipation then turned the brass knob.

Lowering my head, I stepped into the attic which was huge, far larger than I expected, and realised it must run the good length of the house. Looking up I saw the massive oak beams which held the roof in place and my dilemma was where to start.

There were pieces of old furniture, long forgotten chests and pieces of porcelain. I moved across to one table on which stood quite a few pieces of china and picked up a small figurine of a lady dressed in a rose-coloured pink dress with a yellow rose on her shoulder and one in her hair. I recognised this as a piece my grandmother had always kept in the bedroom on the mantel-piece. I placed it back on the table intending to take it with me on my way out.

A thought struck me as I walked slowly across the bare floorboards looking at the various chests. Would I find Lizzie's clothes? The thought spurred me on and I slowly lifted the lid of each chest to no avail.

They contained mainly men's and children's clothing. Frustration was creeping upon me as I neared the end of the attic finding I had to stoop as the roof was much lower here. Cobwebs impeded my path and tangled themselves in my hair, but I pressed on as I'd spied a chest in the corner.

On reaching it, I first had to wipe the dust off with the palm of my hand, as I tried to lift the lid it would not move, but to my delight could see that the key was in the rusty lock. I turned it with some excitement and the lid lifted easily, swinging back on its hinges. I looked at the contents with tears springing to my eyes, for it was indeed Lizzie's clothing.

On top lay a green fur-trimmed hood and cloak, not dissimilar to the green I had worn today. Lovingly I picked it from the chest, holding it in my hands and laying the material against my cheek, Lizzie's perfume still lingered faintly and I took it in breathing deeply.

'Oh, Grandmother,' I whispered aloud, 'How I wish you were here, what's happened to you?' I waited almost expecting a reply, but the attic was silent except for the slight creaking of the floorboards under my feet. Almost reverently I laid the cloak back in the chest, I couldn't bear to see anything else today. Slowly I lowered the lid and turned the key in the lock slipping the key in the side pocket of my dress, not wanting anyone but me to look through Lizzie's things. But by the looks of the cobwebs at this end of the attic no-one had been here for many years.

Stooping even lower, I headed towards a small window at the end for I'd seen the back of a large picture leaning against the wall. On reaching it I pushed the cobwebs away with my hands and tried to lift it to turn it around, nearly dropping it because of its weight.

Full of determination, I placed my hands halfway down each side of the frame and heaving it up and around with a strength I didn't know I had, then placed it with some effort back on the floor. It was my grandmother's portrait, for I recognised the cornflower blue dress and the coal black hair, but to my dismay as I stood looking down at it I could see someone had fiercely slashed at her face with some sharp instrument. As I stood there because of my distress tears streaming down my cheeks, I wondered which malicious person had done this to my beloved Lizzie.

5

A few days passed without incident since I had found my grandmother's portrait. I'd not yet mentioned it to anyone, but at the right moment I intended to tell Aunt Rachel. Many times I'd turned it over in my mind trying to work out who would do such a thing and with such obvious hatred.

Since our visit to the dressmaker's I'd seen little of Gareth. He was either out or shut away in his studio. Consequently, we had not continued to build on our relationship. I had not seen Jared at all and was blissfully unaware that this was about to change.

April was nearly upon us. The warm weather was clement and I was restless. Grace would arrive tomorrow, but until then I needed something to occupy my day.

'What are you to do today?' Pru

asked as she busied herself tidying up my bedroom. Tidiness was not one of my better attributes.

'I'm thinking I may go to Culmoor Church as it is such a beautiful day and maybe explore the graveyard again.' As I spoke I lay the Charles Dickens novel I was reading on the table.

'It will do you good to take your head out of that book, Miss, and get some fresh air. You are looking quite pale lately, now let us get you dressed.'

Pru's words brought to mind the fact that I was still in my night attire, so immediately set to dressing, Pru helping me into a pale pink day dress. She then wrapped a heavy cream lace shawl around my shoulders and helped tie the ribbons on a matching pink wide-brimmed bonnet.

'Will I do?' I asked Pru. Why I asked I didn't know except that at the back of my mind I knew I had to look my best at all times.

'You look perfect. Now run along while I finish tidying up here and then I must go to your mother and see if she will get dressed today.' These words from Pru made me realise I'd not seen Mother for a couple of days as she'd been suffering from one of her bad heads.

'Give her my love, Pru, and please tell her I'll see her later.' Closing the door behind me and making my way along the corridor, to my dismay I saw Jared walking towards the staircase also from the opposite direction. I quickened my step in the hope that I would reach the stairs before him, but we both met on the top step.

'You look lovely today, cousin,' he remarked quietly. As he spoke I looked down into the hall silently praying that someone would be there, but the whole house seemed silent.

'Why thank you, Jared,' I replied making a move to descend, but I was prevented from doing so by Jared turning me to face him.

'Come with me cousin Silvia, for I have something that I wish you to see.'

As he spoke Jared took a firm grip on my arm and led me along the corridor towards the attic stairs taking no heed of my protestations.

'Will you please release me, cousin,' I almost shouted in vain hope that someone would hear. We had stopped in front of the last door on the left, looking at the door I felt a sense of impending gloom.

'This, cousin, is the master bedroom, which if you choose to marry him you will share with my brother.' So saying he turned the brass handle on the door flinging it wide open and dragging me in, only then did he release the strong grip on my arm. And while it was my chance to escape I could not help but stand transfixed to the dark wooden floor and look around me.

The large room held no warmth, the dark blue heavy curtains were drawn blocking out any sunlight, the fireplace was built of slate grey-coloured marble and even with a fire burning I could not image it radiating any warmth. The walls were the same blue as the drawing-room which I loathed. A huge dark mahogany wardrobe filled the wall by the window, and adjacent to the door was an equally large matching four-poster bed carved with grotesque faces.

I stared at it quite forgetting Jared's presence until he spoke, his voice breaking into my almost mesmerised thoughts. 'So cousin, does this little scene thwart any plans you may have of marrying Gareth for the sake of Darkwood? For this is Darkwood in truth, where our grandfather slept and ruled this house and all its occupants with a rod of iron.'

As Jared spoke I could feel myself trembling, but was it with fear or anger? I was outraged at the way Jared had brought me here, but at the same time grateful that he had shown me this hideous room.

There was no way that I'd sleep in this room as it was now, everything would have to be altered from the colour of the walls to the bed. Jared stood to one side of the window, walking swiftly across, I drew back the curtains with defiance as sunlight streamed in making little difference. I had no intention of telling this cousin how I felt about anything for to do so would only serve to raise his hopes.

As I looked at Jared's face I could see the cruel twist of his mouth, so like the one I had seen in the portrait of our grandfather, Samuel, a trait Jared had obviously inherited, and wishing to get away from him as much as the oppressive room, I picked up my skirts and ran back along the corridor, not stopping until I reached the bottom of the staircase.

Taking a few deep breaths to calm myself I looked back towards the staircase, but thankfully Jared had not followed. At this moment Aunt Rachel's voice startled me.

'Silvia dear, where are you going?' she enquired in her soft voice.

'To Culmoor Church as it is a

beautiful day and I wish to go out for a while.' I smiled as I spoke trying to control the tremor in my voice caused by my experience with my aunt's youngest son.

'I cannot let you go unchaperoned Silvia, I would join you myself, but I have a visitor calling later. Leave it until tomorrow when I can accompany you.' Her request was reasonable, but I was stubborn.

'I'm sorry, Aunt, but I have set my heart on going now. As Mother is indisposed I will take Pru.' These words obviously pleased her.

'That will be much more in keeping. We have a guest for dinner this evening, so please don't linger longer than necessary dear. I like to make Estelle feel welcome when she visits.' At Aunt Rachel's words my heart sank. I had hoped not to see the lovely Estelle again until my marriage to Gareth.

'Has she no-one to accompany her?' I asked as sweetly as I could.

'No dear, unfortunately she is all

alone in the world since her mother died.' Aunt Rachel's voice was almost wistful being one to gather lonely people to her bosom and care for them.

'She is extremely pretty, I'm surprised some young man hasn't whisked her to the altar before now.' My voice held the interest I felt and I waited for my aunt's reply which stunned me somewhat.

'Estelle has eyes only for Gareth, and until you and he are married she will not look beyond him.'

The startled expression on my face must have shown for Aunt Rachel tried to pacify me. 'But that doesn't mean that Gareth returns her affection, quite the contrary.' Little did I know that later that day I would recall my aunt's words.

'No matter, I must find Pru for time is pressing,' I said wishing to change the course of the conversation.

'You do that and I shall arrange for Matt to convey you in the pony and trap.' She turned to go and then turned back. ‘By the way, Silvia, there is a letter for you. It is on the chest by the front door, enjoy your outing.’

At Aunt Rachel’s words I hastened over to the chest, picking up the letter. I could see it was Grace’s handwriting. Just as I was about to climb back up the staircase, Dotty was scurrying across the hall, and seeing me she dropped a curtsey. ‘I’m sorry Miss, I’ve been sent to light the fire in the drawing-room,’ she explained.

‘Before you do, Dotty, could you please find my maid, Pru, and ask her to get herself ready to accompany me. I will meet her in the hall in a quarter-of-an-hour,’ I asked, turning to the drawing-room, intent on reading my letter. I preferred not to go upstairs just in case I encountered Jared once more. Dotty didn’t answer, but scurried off in search of Pru.

Sitting on the settle in the cold drawing-room I eagerly opened Grace’s letter which read,

My dearest Silvia,

I am truly sorry to impart bad tidings, but I find I cannot join you this week as planned. My mother is so ill I just cannot leave her at present. I know this will cause you some distress as indeed it does me, but as soon as Mama is stronger I will join you, for I am so longing to see you and Darkwood. Have you set a date for your wedding? Please write soon with your news.

From your loving friend,

Grace.

I read the letter several times, tears springing to my eyes. So Grace would not be here to talk to as I had so hoped and above all else I had no bridesmaid, but I understood that Grace could not leave her sick mother.

When I left the drawing-room, Dotty already had a fire springing to life in the hearth. Pru was waiting for me in the hall dressed in her light brown moreno dress which accentuated the colour of her red hair.

'Miss Silvia, what are we about? I have so many tasks to perform and your mother is quite put out that I should have to leave her.' Pru chattered on hardly allowing me to explain, which I managed to do as we stepped out into the warm spring sunshine and Matt assisted us into the pony and trap.

As we bowled along the narrow lane, I looked back at the house. In the spring sunshine the building looked quite appealing and I caught sight of the bridge which led into the wood beyond. I was soon to be a married woman and no longer under my late grandfather's spell. I would one day very soon venture into the wood and see for myself if it was inhabited by ghouls and goblins.

The thought of Samuel brought to mind the master bedroom at Darkwood and my thought was to speak with Gareth about it at my first opportunity.

Nearly all the way I could see the church perched on top of the small hillock. As we reached the bottom of it I could see the steep path winding its way through the grass and idly wondered how Mother would manage to walk up to the church on my wedding day. As Matt helped me alight on to the path, Pru made to follow, but I stopped her from doing so. 'Please Pru, sit in the sunshine and rest for I wish to go alone.' I coaxed her and could see she was somewhat relieved, as to climb anything was not Pru's favourite pastime.

As I made my way slowly up the uneven path, I realised it wasn't as difficult as I had imagined. Nearing the gate I took a look back at the view behind me. The whole landscape was a field stretching into the distance where I had a glimpse of the sea merging into the blue sky. Passing through the gate, the church loomed up towards me. My thought was that very soon I would walk this way dressed in my wedding gown.

As I walked around the side of the

church to the entrance I could see that the view from here was the same on all sides, grass lay each side of the granite building and one solitary seat stood against the surrounding wall. I stepped out of the sunlight into the dark porch and was glad Pru had the sense earlier to lay a shawl around my shoulders which I pulled tightly around me as I felt suddenly cold.

Lifting the latch on the heavy door and pushing it enough to allow me to pass through, I stepped on to the cold granite slab floor. It was lighter in here for the sun slanted through some of the small plain windows set high in the outer wall, casting rays intermittently across the brown, well worn pews.

The interior of the church was far smaller than I had imagined. Making my way slowly down the aisle I looked up to the colourful window above the altar. It was then I noticed out of the corner of my eye that someone was sitting in the front pew, a man, who had obviously not heard me enter.

I made to retreat, the skirts of my dress catching on the pews as I turned to retrace my steps.

'Cousin Silvia,' the voice startled me and I realised I was caught in a beam of sunlight. My heart started pounding as it dawned on me that the voice belonged to Gareth. As I turned around to face him he said, 'We are of the same mind.'

'We obviously are, cousin.' I managed to stammer. 'I am pleased that I have seen you alone, for there is something I wish to discuss with you.' As I spoke the words I felt foolish, it was all I could think of to say. Gareth looked at me intently, moving towards me until he was so close I could feel his breath on my cheek as he spoke.

'And what would that be, cousin? Our wedding perhaps?' There was a playful gleam in his dark eyes, I noticed that he again wore black which so became him and his eyes glinted in the sun's ray.

'Indirectly yes, cousin, for I cannot,

no will not, sleep in the master bedroom as it is.'

Gareth's expression changed at my words, he looked puzzled. 'And how did you come to view this bedroom, cousin?' he queried in a quite controlled voice.

'Because Jared had great delight in showing it to me this very morning, in truth he almost dragged me in there,' I replied, remembering with clarity the whole scene.

'Did he indeed.' As he spoke Gareth turned away from me so I could not detect the look on his face, but I knew he was displeased. He turned back to me. 'We will change it to your liking cousin, for we cannot have you disliking our marital bedroom, can we? Enjoy your look around, 'tis a pleasant enough place to wed. I will see you at dinner.' With these words and leaving me speechless he strode out of the church and left me.

A little while later I stepped thankfully back into the sunshine. Walking across the grass I sat for a few minutes on the wooden seat savouring the warmth of the sun. Thoughts whirled again in my head, uppermost in my mind were three things. An inattentive bridegroom, his amorous brother and the absence of a bridesmaid. As I mulled this over an idea came to me and I hasted back across the grass through the gate down the path to the pony and trap.

'Home now, Miss?' Matt asked as he helped me back into the trap next to Pru.

'No Matt, I wish to call at the vicarage please, wherever that may be.'

No sooner had I said it, Matt was in his seat skilfully steering the pony and us towards the vicar's abode, which I was to learn was just across from the church.

'Whatever do you want to go there for, Miss Silvia?' Pru was beginning to sound like my mother.

'You will see Pru, I have an idea,' I said as we stopped outside a double-fronted building similar to Lizzie's stitching of the house in her sampler, only instead of being red, this one was grey like the church. The whole place on the outside at least was shabby, paint was peeling from the window sills and the black front door.

I waited for an answer to my knock, and after a little time the door was opened by a pleasant looking elderly woman dressed in a royal blue dress covered by a clean crisp white apron. She looked startled to see me and said, 'Oh Miss, begging your pardon, I expected it to be that young tyke, Jake again, knocking the door and running away, we weren't expecting visitors, the vicar is out, Miss, I'm afraid.'

'It's Isabel I've come to see if she's in, please.' As I spoke I could hear a piano being played rather skilfully from somewhere in the house.

'Come in.' She pulled the door wider to allow me to enter into the shabby looking hall with brown threadbare carpet. 'I take it you're Miss Silvia, I remember you as a child

I do. As pretty then as you are now, if you don't mind me saying.

'Why thank you.' I enthused. 'And you are?' I smiled trying to put her at ease, the piano still playing.

'Sorry Miss, I'm Mrs Ledbetter, been the vicar's housekeeper and cook for over forty years. Not the same vicar I hastened to add, I've seen quite a few come through that door in my time.'

As Mrs Ledbetter spoke she led me to a door on the right at the back of the hall. 'Please go in, Miss.' As I entered the room I could see Isabel sitting at the piano at one corner playing avidly. As soon as she heard me she stopped and stood up, smoothing her hands nervously over the skirts of her dull grey woollen dress. She looked taken aback at seeing me and quite rightly too I thought.

'You play the piano beautifully, Isabel.' I spoke truthfully. A glimmer of a smile hovered on her lips and her eyes showed some animation.

'Thank you,' she replied demurely.

‘I’m sorry, but George is out.’

‘It’s you I’ve come to see, Isabel. I would like you to be my bridesmaid.’ These words provoked a response, one hand flew to her mouth and her eyes opened wide with pleasure. I could now see they were a startling blue, corn-flower blue I thought, as I left the house with instructions that I would call for her at ten o’clock next morning. My intention was to turn this moth into a lovely butterfly.

6

While Pru helped me choose a dress for dinner that evening, my mother walked in and without ceremony sat down in the armchair. She looked tired I thought, and was obviously not joining us for dinner as she was not suitably attired.

'How are you feeling?' I enquired solicitously.

'No matter how many powders I take my head still pounds, but it will pass,' she replied with some optimism. 'Pru tells me you called at the vicarage today. May I ask why?'

'Not to cancel the wedding, Mother, if that's what you are thinking.' I laughed, and continued to select a suitable gown.

'Well, thank the Lord for that at least. So why did you visit?' she asked.

'To ask Isabel if she'd be my

bridesmaid, and she very graciously agreed.' As I spoke I picked out my most daring dress, a creation of lemon coloured silk with a scooped off the shoulder neckline. Small cream coloured flowers decorated the hem and the short puffed sleeves and pointed bodice. My dilemma was should I wear it or not. As I thought of Estelle my mind was made up.

'Silvia, I'm talking to you,' my mother's voice interrupted my thoughts as I handed the dress to Pru. 'Why ask Isabel when you have the lovely Grace?'

'Grace cannot come,' and I handed Mother the letter which she perused while Pru helped me dress. Sitting at the dressing table I clasped cream pearls at my neck and Pru fashioned my dark hair, bunching it up at the back and covering it with a pale lemon snood to match my gown.

As I stood up my mother looked me up and down and then got up with Pru's help. Before leaving the room she asked, 'Why Isabel? Why not Estelle?'

There were many reasons I wasn't about to ask Estelle, but didn't wish to go into that with Mother. 'Because I wish to help Isabel see the beauty in herself. Under that plain silent exterior there is a lovely young woman fighting to get out. She just needs some feminine advice, and tomorrow when I take her to Caroline Peacock in Tavistock we shall see what beauty lies beneath.' I said all this with the hope that this would be an end to it, but my mother had to have the final word.

'The real reason Silvia, I know it and you know it, is that you feel that you cannot compete with the lovely Estelle. I shall come with you on the morrow, enjoy your evening.' As mother left I looked at Pru, exasperation on my face.

'Don't take any notice Miss, it's her head. I know your reasons are as you say, you have a kind heart. Now you'd best get down to dinner.'

Pru's words cheered me and I walked along the corridor with a spring in my step. As I started to walk down the stairs I heard voices to my right. Looking over the banister I could see Gareth and Estelle looking as lovely as ever in a pale pink gown.

Her words drifted up to me, 'Don't marry her, marry me dear Gareth,' she pleaded.

'I cannot Estelle, I have told you so many times,' Gareth replied.

'May I ask why? No, I will give you the answer, it's because of this house, isn't it. You aren't marrying Silvia, you are marrying Darkwood.' Her voice rose with each word. I waited with baited breath, what would be my cousin's reply?

'Keep your voice down please, Estelle. It's true I love this house, it is part of me and my desire to own it is strong, but it isn't the reason I can't marry you.' Gareth's voice was firm.

'Then kiss me at least, Gareth, for I have so much longing for you.' So saying, she reached up to his face with her hands, but Gareth held her at arms' length, gently pushing her away.

'I cannot do that either, Estelle. Forget me, think of me only as a friend.' His voice was soothing like a father to a child.

Miss Benedict stamped her foot and pulled away from him. 'You won't marry her. I promise!' She almost screamed at him.

This is where I must continue my progress down the stairs, I thought. The conversation I'd just heard was most interesting and proved Aunt Rachel to be correct this morning. Gareth looked up as I reached the bottom of the staircase.

'Silvia,' he exclaimed. 'Estelle and I were just about to go into the drawing-room. I hear from mother that you have had some bad news today.

As he spoke, my thought was that he was most courteous this evening, and for the first time had called me by my christian name. The questions burning in my mind were, was my future husband feeling guilty or was he softening towards me? I fervently hoped it was the latter.

* * *

The evening did not go well. At the dinner table each time I glanced at Estelle she was watching me and then returned to flirting outrageously with Jared, who was obviously enjoying the attention and was flirtatious in return.

It was obvious to me that they were both trying to upset Gareth and myself, for my part at least it didn't work. I had no interest in my ruthless cousin. Aunt Rachel watched the pair throughout the meal and Gareth sat opposite me glancing in my direction while we talked with Uncle William. We were all like pawns in a game of chess and I idly wondered who would make the first move. I was to find out the next day that it would be Aunt Rachel.

Next morning after an early breakfast my intention was to seek out my aunt. Walking across the hall smoothing the skirts of the green dress I wore, I encountered Mrs Trigg who told me I would find her in the morning room. I made my way to the corridor which ran to the left at the back of the hall, opening the first door I realised it was a small library, books were stacked neatly around the shelves, four comfortable red armchairs had been placed around a table in the centre of the room.

Thankfully the walls in here had not been painted blue but a deep red to match the furniture, the whole room looking inviting. Closing the door I walked farther down the corridor. The sound of voices slowed me and as I reached the next door I could hear Aunt Rachel's voice. 'I've told you many times before, Estelle is out of bounds to you.' For the second time in as many days I realised I was eavesdropping as my aunt continued, 'You are to stay away from her and that is an order.'

'I'm a man now, not a boy,' came Jared's reply. 'And I shall do as I please.

I notice that you do not admonish Gareth.'

'Gareth adheres to my wishes, and I should be most pleased if you would do likewise.' Aunt Rachel's voice was firmer than I'd ever known it.

'We shall see,' Jared said. 'I don't care for these confusing demands you are making.' As he spoke I realised that he was approaching the door, so gathering myself together I tapped at the door.

On pushing it open I came face to face with my cousin who looked at me and his mother with some disdain, and without so much as a good morning left us. I wondered what kept the lovely Miss Benedict apart from my two cousins.

'Good morning, Silvia.' My aunt's voice sounded softer again. 'You are early today.'

'Yes, Aunt,' I replied looking around this delightful room which was decorated in a soft green, the sun already streaming through the window, a ray of which cast a light on the highly-polished writing bureau at which Aunt Rachel sat.

'Have you any idea where the key is to Grandmother's writing desk?' I continued.

'No, dear, we've never found it. And your grandfather said that nothing was to be touched in that room except for my mother's clothes.' This I had already discovered I thought. 'So why do you ask?' my aunt queried.

'I need to write to Grace,' I replied and knew exactly what Aunt Rachel would say.

'You can use my desk with pleasure, Silvia,' she said rising from her chair and gathering up the papers she was writing on.

'I'd prefer to use my grandmother's, although I thank you for your offer,' I said with a sense of discontent. 'Surely Aunt, now Grandfather is no longer with us the rule no longer applies.'

My aunt looked at me for some seconds before she spoke. 'You are quite right, Silvia. Who am I to prevent you using your grandmother's desk. As we can't find a key, I will send Douglas to your room to lever it open.'

'Oh, thank you,' I said with some joy, running over to my aunt and kissing her cheek.

She smiled. 'And while you are here, Silvia, I have to say we have to organise the invitations for your wedding.'

'Invitations?' I queried. 'Why surely there is no-one to send any to.'

'We need to invite your Great Aunt Annie and her daughter, Constance, and then there is Estelle,' Aunt Rachel explained.

'Oh well,' I conceded. 'Perhaps we should do it now.'

'No, dear, tomorrow will be soon enough, I hear today you are to take Isabel to Tavistock.' I sensed displeasure in my aunt's voice.

'Why yes, I wish to do something nice for her, for her life obviously holds little to interest her other than the piano.' At my words, Aunt Rachel smiled. I knew she would understand for she also had a kind heart.

'May I join you?' she asked.

'Why of course, I'd very much like you to,' I said with enthusiasm. We made to leave and suddenly I turned back to my aunt, a thought occurring to me. 'Aunt Rachel, why has Lizzie's portrait been damaged?'

As I spoke she turned back to me. 'I didn't know it had been,' she said with some concern. 'Did you locate it in the attic?'

'Yes, Aunt, but someone has slashed at your mother's face with some sharp instrument. It quite upset me,' I said, a tremor in my voice as I recalled the day I had found it.

'I will look into it,' my aunt said, squeezing my hand. 'Let it not spoil our visit to the dressmaker. I will ask Douglas to come up to your room on our return. Now let us get ready.'

Duly we collected Isabel as promised. I noted that she had made some effort to look her best. She wore a pale blue worsted dress with a black lace collar, a blue cameo brooch pinned to the neck and a black shawl across her shoulders. The black bonnet decorated with blue flowers which she wore, suited her, and as she smiled at me on entering the carriage I realised that I was right, she had a pretty face and given the right circumstances would look quite enchanting.

'How fortuitous, Miss Harvey,' enthused Caroline Peacock as she let us into her establishment once more. 'Your gown is ready for fitting.'

'Fortuitous indeed,' I replied. 'But first I need to choose material for my bridesmaid,' I said, leading Isabel forward. Caroline looked her up and down and went to lead us into a different room from our previous visit, but I stopped her.

'No Miss Peacock, I wish to choose a silk for Isabel, a blue silk to match her eyes.'

'Why yes, of course Miss Harvey, quite appropriate.' And she led us into the room holding the bales of silk, while Mother and Aunt Rachel looked on, I chose a beautiful cornflower blue which I'd spotted before.

'This will be admirable. Do you agree, Isabel?' I said to her seeing her eyes light up with pleasure as she touched it.

'Oh, thank you, Miss Silvia. I can hardly believe my good fortune,' she said, and nor could Caroline Peacock I thought, as we were taken to the fitting room. While Isabel was measured, I instructed Caroline that I wished her to have a gown similar to mine which Miss Peacock agreed.

'Now let us try your gown.' So saying she led me behind a wooden screen. Aunt Rachel assisted me while my mother sat on a chair in the corner. Caroline returned with another young woman carrying my wedding gown.

As I saw the ivory silk laying across their arms, I felt a great sense of anticipation which I had not expected to feel. The skirt of the dress which must have held yards of material was placed over my head falling perfectly over my hooped petticoat, the back was secured with hooks and eyes then the fitted whale bone pointed bodice was put on by Caroline, after which the young woman did up the many hooks and hand stitched eyes at the front.

The silk felt soft on my arms and I suddenly seemed like a different person. As I looked in the full-length mirror I had the desire to twirl around as the effect was astounding. With my lace veil and flowers I would be fit to marry a king.

'You look beautiful, Silvia,' my mother and aunt both observed in unison, their hands covering their cheeks with obvious emotion. As I looked down at the shimmering skirt I could see the braid showing a little below the hem to preserve it and the long-sleeved bodice fitted my figure perfectly, my hair seeming even darker in contrast to the ivory of the gown. I was captured in the moment and felt a sudden longing to walk down the aisle to Gareth, but alas I had two more weeks to wait.

'You are pleased with the result, Miss Harvey?' Caroline's voice cut into my thoughts and I was transported back to the present.

'Absolutely delighted,' I enthused. 'I thank you and your seamstresses from the bottom of my heart.'

'We should remove it now,' Caroline said, 'as we need to do the finishing touches.'

'One moment,' I said as I thought of Isabel and walked out from behind the screen, the skirts of the gown moving as in one with me. Isabel had been sitting on a chair wearing her bonnet ready for our departure.

At the sight of me she stood up, walked slowly towards me then around me. 'You look so lovely, Miss Silvia. Am I really to wear a gown similar to this?' she asked, a pleasing smile lit up her face and her eyes sparkled.

'Indeed you are,' I replied. 'You will

look lovely, and I'm so glad to witness such enthusiasm, you will make an admirable bridesmaid.'

'I promise I shall do my best, Miss. You are most kind.' As Isabel spoke I knew that the smile now would not vanish as she had something to look forward to. I could have hugged her, but decorum and Miss Peacock hovering around me obviously protective of her creation prevented me from doing so.

As we left, Caroline said that she would deliver both gowns to Darkwood in ten days time, bringing her senior seamstress in case there were any alteration needed on Isabel's gown.

I felt the whole morning had been a success and on the way back to Darkwood could think of no-one but Gareth. On our arrival back at Darkwood as if in answer to my thoughts as we stepped into the hall, I could see Gareth was waiting for us, lounging lazily at ease in one of the armchairs. At the sight of us he stood up and walked towards me.

'Silvia, I wish to speak with you alone.' As he spoke I looked around at my mother and aunt but they showed no opposition to this, so Gareth continued. 'In view of your dislike of blue walls, I suggest to talk in my mother's morning room.' As he spoke he made for me to follow him which I did like a lamb, my only wish was that I'd had a chance to refresh myself, but Gareth was, I realised, one who would catch the moment.

As I entered the morning-room for the second time in one day, I thought how restful this room was and that Gareth had chosen well.

'Please remove your bonnet, Silvia,' Gareth said quietly. I did as I was bid and laid it on a table by the door. 'Now please sit in the chair by the mantel.' He indicated a small green armchair between the window and the fireplace. I sat decorously on the edge of my chair, smoothing the skirt of my green dress around me and wondering what this was all about. Gareth knelt on one knee before me and opened a red velvet box which contained a ruby and diamond ring.

The light from the window caught the stones and as I looked at them with some fascination and awe they sparkled back at me, the sight of it held my attention for some moments and then I looked at Gareth's handsome face as he spoke, 'Will you marry me, Silvia?' His words were so unexpected I was speechless. 'I'm asking you to be my wife,' he continued.

'Yes Gareth, I will marry you.' My heart sang, and for my part at least my words were sincere. As he took my left hand and gently placed the ring on my finger, I knew I was falling in love with this handsome unpredictable man who was to be my husband, and I fervently wished with all my being that one day he could feel the same.

As he stood up I could see a satisfied look on his face as he smiled down at me. 'You can stand up now, Silvia,' and taking my hand he pulled me to my feet. 'I think a kiss would be appropriate to seal our betrothal.' Without warning he drew me to him and bending towards me our lips met briefly for the first time.

His mouth was gentle on mine and I savoured the brief moment feeling quite bereft when he released me, his eyes sparkled as he looked down at me and I was sure something unspoken hovered on his lips.

'We have lingered long enough, Silvia.' The moment was gone and his voice brought me back to the present, as he gently lifted my left hand, looking at the ring he'd only moments ago placed on my finger. 'Wear it well, lovely lady, for it is the Hunter betrothal ring and not given lightly.'

'I will treasure it I promise, and to say I am honoured does not do my feelings justice.' Thankfully I had at last found my tongue and as I spoke I wondered how my cousin would feel if he knew the extent of my feelings for him. But I realised that for the moment at least words I longed to say to him would need to be held in abeyance.

As we left the room and we made our way together to the hall, I glanced back at the green chair by the fireplace and thought it would forever be one of my favourite places.

The ruby ring burned delightfully into my hand. As we reached the bottom of the staircase the front door burst open and Estelle stood there dressed in an emerald green riding habit. She looked at us and striding towards us tapping her riding crop against her skirt, I was mesmerised by the wild look in her green eyes and the pure hatred etched on her beautiful face.

Without a word of warning she lashed out with her riding crop intent on lashing at my face, but Gareth caught it in one hand saving me from injury.

'What are you doing, Estelle?' he said as he removed the crop from her grasp.

I noticed blood on his hand where the whip had cut into his palm.

'I find out today, that she!' Estelle screamed pointing a finger in my direction, 'She has asked someone else to be her bridesmaid!' As I looked at the wildness in her eyes I thought she was either jealous to the point of distraction or unstable.

As I climbed up the stairs to my room, leaving Gareth to calm her I also thought that the whole unpleasant incident had completely spoiled what had been the most beautiful morning of my life.

7

I closed my bedroom door behind me and leaned against it, many thoughts tumbling through my head. Since I'd arrived at Darkwood, so many things had happened in a short space of time.

I couldn't find Lizzie's final resting place which irked me somewhat. Nor could I imagine who could have so wilfully damaged my dear grandmother's portrait and I felt helpless as I had no way of finding out. My only hope was that Aunt Rachel would eventually throw some light on the mystery which beset me, and why did Aunt Rachel forbid Gareth and Jared to associate with Estelle?

This was in itself another mystery which led me to think of the lovely Estelle's outburst in the hall, and I pondered over what the outcome would have been if Gareth had not been there to save me. Then the thought of Gareth brought to mind his proposal. Why had he done it? I chose to think he now wished to marry me, but in truth I was sure it was just a gallant gesture on his part to help me feel better about our forthcoming union, and if this was the reason then he was at least a gentleman.

The thought consoled me somewhat and I walked over to Lizzie's writing desk. Just as I reached it, the door opened and Aunt Rachel stepped in, accompanied by Douglas.

'I brought Douglas up to see if he could open the desk.' As my aunt spoke I could see that Douglas had a small flat metal lever in his hand. While he gently manoeuvred it in the lock, Aunt Rachel and I looked on.

What must she be thinking I wondered, and was somewhat surprised it hadn't been tried before. For my part I was just anxious to see what my grandmother's desk held. After a couple of minutes, the front of the bureau fell down with a sudden jolt and the interior was at last revealed.

'You won't be able to shut it properly, Miss,' Douglas said to my aunt. 'A new lock would be the answer. I'll set to finding one right now.' With these words he left us. Both of us just stood and looked, neither of us willing to be the first to touch anything. At that moment Aunt Rachel made a decision.

'I'm going to leave you, Silvia, to look through the contents and I trust that if there is anything at all of importance you will bring it to me.'

'But of course, Aunt Rachel, I promise.' As I spoke I reached out with my left hand to pick up a sheet of cream coloured paper which lay on its own outside the tiny compartments and pigeonholes of the desk. As I looked down I saw the ruby ring flash in the light from the window. I looked at my aunt and could see by the look on her face that she was aware of it also.

'Why, Silvia, you are wearing the betrothal ring. Did Gareth give this to you?' Her voice held surprise.

'Yes, Aunt, he did,' I replied almost sheepishly. 'Only a short time ago in the morning room.'

'To say I am delighted is the truth,' my aunt said in a quiet voice. 'For Gareth had thought to present you with it on your wedding day. Does this mean . . . ' Her voice trailed off, and I knew the reply I could give her was not the one she hoped for.

'It really doesn't mean anything, Aunt.' As I spoke the expression on her face changed to one of disappointment. 'But I can tell you, for my part at least, I am warming to your son. The very fact that he has given me this lovely token of our forthcoming marriage shows that he is no longer so adverse to it, don't you think?' I could see the words pleased her as my aunt smiled.

'Indeed, it would seem to be so and I am delighted, for you are a lovely gentle young woman. My wish is that given time, you and Gareth will be blissfully happy together. Now I must leave you and I will see you at dinner unless you have anything to show me.' So saying she kissed my cheek before leaving me to look through the desk.

In truth there appeared to be little of significance in it. I held the piece of paper in the light that fell from the window and three-quarters of the way down could make out the name, Lizzie, where the indentation of a pen on the previous sheet had left an imprint, but I could make out little else. I picked up the pen which was tucked in one of the compartments, the nib of which was stained with dry blue ink. As I held it in my left hand, for I was left-handed as Lizzie had been, I imagined her holding it and writing a letter as the sun fell on her smooth skin.

Maybe she'd written to some relative in Ireland whom she perhaps never saw again, or had she written invitations for people to dine at Darkwood? Whatever she had done, I wished so much that she were here with me now. I laid the pen back in its rightful place, not wishing to change a thing. Other small cubicles just held paper and envelopes.

On the left at the back was a small drawer with a tiny wooden handle. I gently pulled it open. Inside lay a neatly folded sheet of the cream coloured paper. As I slowly unfolded it, the creases had left their mark across the words written on it, but I could make out that it was a poem. Taking it to the light, I read,

I see the bluebells softly lie,
A carpet of blue to walk upon
and feel,
The beauty of this wood is real.
In April only do they flower,
But through the year, my mind's
picture could,
Capture the tranquil peace of the
bluebell wood.

I looked at it for some moments, tears pricking at my eyes, for the words revealed Lizzie's love of the wood at bluebell time. I had to see it now for myself, but must first take this poem to show Aunt Rachel.

Swiftly I took my cream shawl out of the wardrobe drawer and hastily laid it around my shoulders, my feet spurred on by Lizzie's poignant words. As I hurried down the hallway in search of Aunt Rachel, I could see some activity in the opposite corridor which distracted me, causing me to walk into Pru who dropped the linen she carried.

'Oh, Miss Silvia, now look what you've made me do,' Pru complained. 'Wherever are you off to in such a hurry?' As she spoke, she bent down and gathered up the articles she'd been carrying.

'Pru, I am so sorry,' I said with true contrition. 'I'm in search of my aunt.'

'She can be found with your mother in the drawing-room, taking tea,' said Pru breathlessly as she stood up, the said articles over one arm, albeit not so neatly.

'Thank you, Pru,' I called as I made my way down the stairs. Crossing the hall, I thought briefly of the unpleasant incident with Estelle. Could it really have been only a couple of hours since? As I entered the drawing-room, I could see Mother and my aunt sipping tea and partaking of tasty looking splits with jam and clotted cream which made me realise how hungry I was, not having eaten since breakfast.

'Why, Silvia!' Aunt Rachel exclaimed, 'I had not expected to see you so soon. Sit and join us.' I did as she bid, not needing much coaxing, and immediately started to spoon jam and cream on to the split in my hand while Aunt Rachel rang the bell for another cup and saucer which Dotty brought within minutes.

'It's good to see you back downstairs, Mother,' I remarked as this morning I'd not had much time to speak to her. Was it really only this morning that we'd visited the dressmaker's and I'd tried on my wedding gown?

'So what has brought you so quickly to find us? For I can see you are flushed with excitement from some discovery,'

Mother asked in a booming voice. I reached into the side pocket of my dress, retrieving the piece of paper I'd found with their mother's verse on it.

'I found this,' I said triumphantly. 'It is beautiful.'

Mother took it from me and read it, then silently handed it to Aunt Rachel. Watching them both intently, I could see that Lizzie's words had more effect on my aunt. Her eyes glistened with unshed tears as she looked at it and I felt a greater affinity to her than I ever had with my mother who had always been a selfish person, whereas Aunt Rachel was kind and gentle and always thinking of others.

'It is quite lovely, Silvia. I must confess I had not known that my mother had written it,' said my aunt. 'But I knew your grandmother loved the time of year when the bluebells flowered. She would walk to the wood after luncheon every day when they were out. Here, Silvia, keep it.' As she spoke, Aunt Rachel pressed the piece of paper back into my hand and I placed it back into my pocket.

'Are the bluebells out now?' I asked for I had a great desire to see this bluebell wood.

'Yes, they should be, dear, although I have to admit I have not been in the wood recently,' answered my aunt, picking up her cup and saucer once more. She was obviously trying to take her mind off her recent emotion.

'Then is it all right for me to walk down there alone?' I ventured, getting to my feet.

'Good Lord, child, of course it is. You are old enough to know now that there are no goblins to frighten you,' Mother answered quite harshly I thought, as Aunt Rachel smiled at me. I needed no further encouragement.

As I stepped outside the front door, I stood for some moments savouring the warmth of the sun on my face. It was truly a glorious day with not a cloud in the sky. I tried to imagine which way my grandmother would have walked to the wood. Some instinct told me to stick to the path close to the house, so this is the route I took.

The path was in shade, and out of the sun it felt quite cool. As I reached the end of the house, the sun's rays warmed me once more as I continued walking towards the small bridge. There was a lightness in my step as I reached the curve of the bridge and I stopped for some minutes to look down at the River Dart gurgling merrily over large stones and small pebbles.

The sun felt hot on my back, so I moved on and after a few paces stepped off the bridge on to the grass which felt pleasantly springy under my feet. I turned to look back at Darkwood.

The upper windows sparkled in the afternoon sun and my thought was how different it looked from the March day we arrived here just two-and-a-half weeks ago.

I felt quite drawn to the house now I was older, probably because my grandfather, Samuel no longer ruled it. I shuddered at the thought of him and walked quickly on towards the wood. As I reached the edge of it, my breath was quite taken away and I stopped in my tracks at the beautiful sight which lay before me.

Bluebells grew in abundance, covering the ground with a breathtaking blue carpet for as far as the eye could see, and I understood completely Lizzie's love for this glorious sight. A narrow path formed itself between the flowers and I started to follow it, looking around me. It was cold as the sun didn't quite penetrate through the stunted grey oak trees. They looked almost dead, with long, thick grey branches extending like huge creepers, some tangling together and I suddenly felt afraid.

Feeling sure I was being followed for I heard a twig snap behind me on the path, I turned around to see Jared walking towards me. At the sight of him my heart sank. Looking around I could see no way of escape but to trample over the bluebells.

'Jared,' I exclaimed sweetly, 'Is this coincidence or are you following me?'

'The latter would be more correct,' he said in a quiet, controlled voice. 'I observed you from a window and thought to see what you were about.'

'I just wish to see the wood, and especially the carpet of bluebells,' I replied meekly, looking at his immaculate dark blue jacket and matching waistcoat and a crisp white shirt. His hair was tousled by the slight, cool breeze and his pale blue eyes were cold and calculating as he weighed up the situation which was, I realised with some dismay, that we were alone, some way from the house. I didn't trust this cousin, recalling the day when he had almost dragged me to the master bedroom against my will. I found myself in an unenviable position.

'As a child you refused to come here.' As he spoke, Jared moved towards me and I took a step back, not wishing to be any closer to him. 'You are surely not afraid of me, cousin?' He laughed and moved swiftly nearer to me, catching my wrist in his cold grasp.

As I tried to free myself, the shawl I wore fell to the ground and I realised I was treading on the bluebells. I could hear them squelch under my feet. Jared was backing me against a snarled grey tree trunk. I felt the bark almost pierce into my back as he pushed his body up against me.

I screamed, knowing it was to no avail as he clamped his free hand across my mouth. My heart was pounding and although cold, I could feel the sweat on my brow.

'Just one kiss, cousin, and you will be mine.' His voice was quietly menacing as he spoke and his eyes looked directly into mine, so I closed them tightly as I did not wish to look at his leering face.

'What are you doing, brother?' Gareth's angry voice was music to my ears. A relieved sob escaped my lips as I opened my eyes in time to see Gareth bring his hand up sharply across Jared's face. 'Now go home!' my gallant knight said between clenched teeth. 'And never again touch or go near my betrothed or I will not be responsible for my actions. Believe me, brother, you have escaped lightly.' Jared looked at us both then retreated back towards Darkwood.

Gareth turned to me and with one strong arm pulled me towards him. My head on his shoulder, small sobs escaped me, more with relief than anything as Gareth's hand smoothed my hair gently. Calming down, I lifted my head and looked at him.

'I can't thank you enough,' I said quietly, lifting my hand to touch his cheek. 'I dread to think of my fate had you not chanced to walk this way.'

'It was no chance, I assure you,' he explained. 'I watched you walk and linger on the bridge. As you stepped into the wood, I spied Jared following you and knew from past experience his intentions would not be honourable.'

'You are right in that assumption.' As I spoke I noticed I had at last stopped trembling. Gareth went across to the path and picked up my shawl. Bringing it back, he placed it gently around my shoulders.

'Do you feel better?' he enquired, cupping my chin in his hand.

'I do, except I am concerned about all the bluebells we have trampled on,' I said as I looked around our feet.

'Do not worry, Silvia, there are plenty more.' As he spoke he turned around, one arm conveying the carpet of blue. I smiled as I tried desperately to secure the pins back in my hair which was already falling in disarray around my shoulders. 'Leave it,' Gareth said. 'You have such beautiful hair, it is a sin to hide it.' At his words, my cheeks flushed and I hope he hadn't noticed my confusion.

'Tell me, Silvia, what caused you to walk in the wood alone? I recall as a child, tales of ghosts prevented you from doing so.' As he spoke Gareth looked down at me, a gentle look on his face.

'It is true. When we were children I was afraid to come here, not only because of yours and Jared's tales of ghosts and goblins, but also our grandfather forbade it.' I stopped, thinking back to Samuel's hold over me and I realised even more how much Jared was like him.

'Have no fear, my love, cousin Jared will not approach you again, you have my word as a gentleman,' he assured me.

'I do trust this is true, and in answer to your question, I found this poem today, written by our grandmother. On reading it, I had a sudden, urgent desire to see her bluebell wood.' As I spoke I pulled the piece of paper from my pocket, thankful that after the recent encounter with Jared it was still intact.

I handed it to Gareth who read it. After some time he spoke, 'Poignant words from a grandmother who loved poetry as much as we do.' He handed

Lizzie's poem back to me. 'Let us walk.'

As we walked in a companionable silence, I realised what was missing. No birds sang here and none sat on the grey branches of the trees. I could see it was getting lighter and that we were nearly at the other side of the wood.

I stopped and looked up at his handsome face.

'Gareth, do you know where our grandmother, Lizzie is buried? I scoured the churchyard on the day of our arrival, but could find no trace of a headstone with her name upon it.'

'I have no idea,' he replied softly. 'It is as if she vanished off the face of the earth. It is as much a mystery to me as yourself. Mother will not talk of it and I have pressed her many times on the subject, for I loved my gentle grandmother.'

'Likewise,' I replied with some emotion at Gareth's words. This was another thing we had in common.

'One day soon we will walk through the graveyard together, for two pairs of eyes may be better than one.' His words pleased me. To know he wished to spend time in my company made me realise that he was now in some way closer to me.

Suddenly I became aware of my surroundings, the moor stretched away in the distance, the scenery reminded me of the view seen from Culmoor Church. It was hard to imagine how a wood had appeared in the middle of the moor.

'What are you thinking?' Gareth's words drifted across to me.

'I am unable to understand how a wood like this came to be in the middle of Dartmoor?'

'Not wishing to alarm you further, Silvia, legend has it that the devil planted the trees and gallops through here each night on the stroke of midnight. But have no fear, it is but folklore.' As he spoke I looked back at the wood and was startled to find I recognised this end of it and I searched my mind as to why I should.

The answer came to me suddenly. It was where Samuel Hunter, our grandfather, had had his portrait painted which now hung at the top of the staircase at Darkwood.

'Your thoughts, Silvia?' Gareth asked.

'This is where our grandfather had his portrait painted,' I replied, and Gareth nodded in agreement.

'Let us return to the house, Silvia, for the sun is falling and I don't wish you to catch a chill.' At Gareth's words I pulled my shawl tighter around my shoulders and taking the arm he offered, we retraced our steps back to Darkwood.

As I snuggled my face into the pillow that night, I thought what a long eventful day it had been and certainly one of mixed fortunes. I drifted off to sleep with a picture of the bluebell wood in my mind and Gareth's gallant acts in saving me twice that day. I recalled him calling me 'my love', and my last thought was that I could hardly wait to be his wife.

8

The Sunday morning following that eventful day, we were all to attend church as it was the third time our banns of marriage would be called. Gareth had attended on his own the two previous Sundays, but today there would be a family gathering including myself and with the exception of my mother, who said that she was saving her strength to walk up to the church on my wedding day.

The invitations had been sent out to a great aunt and cousin I didn't know at Lydford and one to Estelle, who to date, had not responded. With only a handful of people it would be a quiet wedding, but none the less important.

Isabel and I felt some anticipation as our gowns would be delivered on Tuesday. We were a trifle concerned as my veil, headdress and silk boots had not yet arrived, but as Aunt Rachel had so rightly said yesterday, there were still seven days to go.

Pru helped me choose a dress for the morning's outing to church while I stood in only a bodice and hooped petticoat. 'What about this one, Miss Silvia?' said Pru as she took from the wardrobe a pale mauve walking dress.

'I think, Pru, it is admirable and I shall wear a matching cloak and bonnet.' As I spoke I realised my arms were cold. The fire had not been lit that morning and looking out of the window I could see only grey skies.

A fleeting thought crossed my mind, that I hoped the weather would be more favourable on our wedding day. Suitably attired, I stood in the hall waiting for the others.

Uncle William appeared first looking quite fetching in a loose grey striped jacket and matching trousers. 'Silvia, my dear, you look charming,' he said, walking across to me and kissing my cheek. I smiled back at him. 'You seem far more relaxed than on the day of your arrival,' he observed.

'You are so right, Uncle. Whereas I dreaded the whole charade, I now look forward so much to my forthcoming marriage to Gareth,' I replied with honesty.

'That is grand,' he said, just as Aunt Rachel, accompanied by Gareth, entered the hall to join us. My heart leapt at the sight of my future husband. He was indeed very handsome, dressed today in a dark grey jacket and trousers with a pale mauve shirt. Pru had indeed chosen my outfit well. Aunt Rachel looked lovely in a pale grey silk dress with matching cloak and bonnet.

'We should be gone.' Uncle William's voice interrupted my thoughts of Gareth and I realised I was gazing at my betrothed with adoring eyes. Thankfully he seemed not to notice. We all stepped on to the path outside the house and into the carriage. Gareth sat next to me as on the day I had first visited Caroline Peacock's dressmaking establishment, but today I felt far more relaxed and unconcerned at his nearness.

Gareth's hand steadied me as we walked up the path to the church gate, villagers were headed this way, too, all dressed in their Sunday best. Some of the men touched their caps in acknowledgement of us.

As we stepped into the church porch the men removed their hats. We walked down the aisle to the first pew which was obviously reserved for the Hunter family as it had been left vacant. I could see Isabel sat at the small organ on one side of the altar. Seeing her I smiled and she smiled back, her whole face lighting up as she did so.

The vicar appeared and we all stood to sing the first hymn, during which there was a commotion at the back of the church. I looked around to see Jared and Estelle walking down the aisle. On reaching the front of the church they settled in the adjacent pew. Jared glanced across at the four of us conveying a look of total defiance.

Throughout the service, Aunt Rachel who was sitting next to me kept leaning across to observe the two of them. Jared looked back at her with a cruel twist to his mouth. I perceived Aunt Rachel was longing to say something, but in view of our surroundings, was forced to keep silent. Someone else, however, we were all to learn, would not keep so silent.

The moment had arrived for the publishing of the banns before the sentences for the offertory.

The vicar stepped forward saying, 'I publish the banns of marriage between Gareth Samuel Hunter and Silvia Eliza Harvey of Darkwood. If any of you know cause or just impediment why these two persons should not be joined in Holy Matrimony, ye are to declare it. This is the third time of asking.'

The church was silent. Gareth and I looked at each other and smiled, then a voice broke the silence.

'I have just cause why they should

not be married.' Estelle's measured and melodic voice echoed around the church. My heart started racing as she stepped forward from her seat to face the congregation.

George Poulter looked lost for words, but suddenly found his voice amidst the ensuing silence. He stepped forward only inches from Gareth to face the bewitching Estelle.

'My child, can you explain your reason for this interruption?' the vicar said with a slight quiver in his voice.

'Indeed I can, Vicar.' She turned to face Gareth, pointing a gloved finger in his direction, 'This man, Gareth Samuel Hunter, is already promised to me!'

Estelle's voice rose with each word and I recalled the evening at Darkwood when she had implored Gareth to marry her.

I felt Gareth's body stiffen beside me. Someone in the congregation coughed loudly.

'So what have you to say, Gareth?'

She almost screamed, her eyes staring wildly at him.

'Madam, you know as well as I, that this is not true and never has been.' His voice was gentler than expected under the circumstances, but I could tell Gareth was struggling to keep his self-control.

'Come now, Miss Benedict,' George Poulter's voice seemed more assured now. 'This obviously is not true, for a gentleman such as Mr Hunter would admit to it. Take your seat,' he coaxed gently, taking her arm, but Estelle wrenched her arm away from him.

'Take my seat, indeed! I will not, and Gareth shall never marry this woman!'

Speaking almost hysterically, she flew at Gareth without warning, intent on scratching his face, but he turned away just in time and she pounded with her fists at his chest. He gently pushed her away and she collapsed at his feet sobbing hysterically. There was no doubt she was unstable in the mind and I felt some pity for her.

It was Aunt Rachel who helped Gareth bring her to her feet and lead her out of the church, all eyes agog at the spectacle they had witnessed. Gareth took his place back beside me and gently laid his hand across mine.

The vicar gathered himself together and spoke quietly to us. 'Gareth, I should by rights defer the wedding, but I can see the unfortunate state of mind Miss Benedict is in, so will let it pass,' he said.

'Thank you,' Gareth and I uttered in one accord.

On arrival back at Darkwood I was somewhat calmer, but Gareth recommended a brandy which I partook in the drawing-room.

'You do believe me, don't you, Silvia?' he asked as I sipped at the brandy.

'I do indeed, Gareth, have no fear. Is Estelle unsound of mind?' I questioned.

'Yes, she is, but I can say no more now.' Little did I know then that I would not see the lovely Estelle Benedict again.

As I stepped back into the hall I could see Mother almost running down the stairs, 'Silvia, Silvia!' She called my name with some excitement in her voice. 'Silvia, where have you been and where is Aunt Rachel?'

'Mother, calm yourself,' I admonished. 'Whatever's wrong?'

'Your parcels have arrived, Silvia, from Honiton and France. I can hardly contain myself and am longing to see your veil. Come child, they are in your room.' So saying, she started back up the stairs with me not far behind her.

As I stopped and looked back at the hall Gareth was stood by the drawing-room door with a glass in his hand and as I caught his eye he raised the glass and smiled.

My purpose was now more assured than ever. As I stepped into my room there was a sense of great excitement.

'I put the packages on your bed,

Miss,' said Pru, walking quickly that way.

'Let me at least remove my bonnet and cloak,' I said, and I did with Pru's help.

'Oh, come on, Silvia!' said Mother, exasperation in her voice. 'And where is your aunt?'

'I am here, Hannah.' Aunt Rachel's voice broke in, she was obviously as full of anticipation as everyone else, and no-one would have known but her and I about the stressful moments of the past couple of hours that we'd endured.

As we all surrounded my bed I could see a long white box and two smaller pink ones. The first box obviously held my veil and I undid the lid with trembling fingers, removing the layers of tissue paper quickly to reveal my Honiton lace veil.

'Take it out of its box, child,' said Mother impatiently as I stood for some seconds looking at it. I did as I was bid and gently removed the full veil from its box, shaking it with care. I ran my hand over the fine white machine net, tracing with my fingers the pillow made lace motifs invisibly sewn to the foundation. It was beautiful and would complement my plain gown perfectly.

Mother, Aunt Rachel and Pru all touched it briefly with a reverent silence and awe before I laid it back in the box.

The next box contained my waxed orange blossom headdress. I took it out of the box amid cries of, 'Try it on, Silvia', so I placed it on my dark hair and ran over to look in the wardrobe mirror, Mother following with the veil which she draped over the headdress.

'It complements your dark hair perfectly,' offered Aunt Rachel, 'You look quite lovely.' And her voice wavered as she spoke.

'I must remove it,' I said, suddenly fearing I would spoil the veil before my wedding day. Mother removed the veil and Pru the headdress, placing them back in their boxes. Aunt Rachel brought the final box over as I sat in Lizzie's armchair. How I wished she were here now, and I wondered if it was possible she was still alive, but I was sure it was just wishful thinking on my part.

'Try these on, Silvia.' Aunt Rachel's voice interrupted my thoughts of Lizzie.

'Let me remove your boots.' As she spoke, Pru helped to remove them while I held the ivory silk half-boots in my hand. The laces were of silk also, and small eyelet holes had been fashioned for them. The small wood block heel was also covered in silk. They were exquisite and a joy to look upon, and thankfully, fitted.

The items all put away and the excitement over, Mother and Aunt Rachel left me to go down to luncheon. I declined as I felt a great tiredness had come over me. The events of the morning had taken their toll. I sank gratefully back into the armchair as Pru went to the kitchen to fetch me some lunch. After eating little, I dozed off to sleep only to be awoken by a gentle tap on my door.

'Come in,' I called sleepily. The door opened to reveal Gareth standing in the doorway and I, suddenly alert, thinking of the last time he had come to my room and hadn't even had the courtesy to knock. The situation had definitely changed since then, but what to, I asked myself, love or respect. The word love had not been spoken and this is what I longed to hear.

'I'm sorry to disturb you,' he said moving further into the room. 'Would you be able to join me now? For I have something which I wish to show you.'

'But of course, just let me place the guard by the fire,' I replied.

I walked with him along the corridor to the far end and I knew for certain he was taking me to the master bedroom. On reaching the door he opened it and bade me enter before him.

As I stepped inside the room, I gasped with surprise, and my hands flew to my mouth. It looked a different room.

The walls were a dusky pink as were

the curtains and bed hangings. Gone was the huge dark mahogany wardrobe and in its place a lighter coloured one. A plush pink carpet decorated with yellow rosebuds covered the floor and a fire was burning cheerfully in the marble grate.

'You are pleased, Silvia?' Gareth asked.

'Indeed I am,' replied, looking back at him. 'I can't quite take it all in.'

'See,' he said, walking into the room, 'I have had a dressing table placed under the window for you, and through here,' as he spoke he opened a door in the far corner which I had not even noticed. As I followed him to look, I could see it contained a hip bath with fluffy white towels on a hand rail.

'You've thought of everything,' I conceded.

'So you could sleep in here after our wedding?' At his words my cheeks grew hot at the thought of our wedding night and I turned back to the bedroom to cover my confusion, asking myself the question he'd just asked. Everything seemed so matter of fact and devoid of emotion, it would indeed be a marriage of convenience. Gareth, by the window, looked at me expecting a reply.

'Yes, I think I could,' was all I would say.

As I walked back along the corridor to my room I felt sorely disillusioned and questioned whether I was doing the right thing. Gareth had gained more than one opportunity of taking me in his arms and speaking of love. The fact that he had not done so led me to believe that he felt nothing other than a desire to inherit this house.

* * *

Tuesday arrived and so did Caroline Peacock with her senior, Mistress Harriet Ford, together with the gowns and work basket. Isabel also arrived and I took her up to my bedroom where we would try on our wedding outfits. Pru was there to assist us and ready to fetch my mother and Aunt Rachel when the gowns were in place.

We removed our outer clothing and Caroline arranged my gown while Harriet dressed Isabel in hers. When we were ready I turned to look at Isabel in her cornflower blue silk. She looked totally enchanting. A smile added to that enchantment and Pru had arranged her hair in a chignon and decorated it with silk flowers to match her gown. Pru then went to fetch the other ladies.

'You must try your headdress and veil,' Mother said. 'We need to see the total effect, don't we, Rachel?' Aunt Rachel agreed and between them placed my headdress on and arranged the beautiful veil.

'Now both of you, stand in front of the mirror,' ordered Mother. Isabel and I did as we were bid. The picture which stared back at us seemed almost unreal. A bride who didn't seem like me at all and a beautiful bridesmaid in a blue which complemented the wedding gown perfectly.

'Oh, Miss Silvia, I can hardly believe it is me,' Isabel declared. As for myself I was pleased the veil covered my face for tears sprung to my eyes as I thought of Gareth and how much I loved him, a love which I knew he did not return, idly wondering at the same time what flowers he would choose for our wedding posies, as it was tradition for the bridegroom to present his bride with the flowers she carried and I also wondered what his feelings were for, alas, he had not proclaimed them to me.

That evening after dinner, I sat in Lizzie's armchair looking at my wedding gown which hung from the picture rail by the door, the flames from the fire casting eerie shadows across it, at times appearing that someone other than I wore it. Then I thought of Isabel and how pleased she was at being my bridesmaid and how lovely she had looked in the cornflower blue gown. What would she do when the wedding was over?

I fervently hoped she would not revert to her solemn ways. Maybe I could help by giving her some company to ensure she wouldn't be disinterested in life again and she could teach me the piano. I'd never play as well as her, but I could make some endeavour for her sake. Estelle came to mind and the outbursts I'd witnessed in recent days. She needed help, this I knew with certainty and pledged to assist all I could.

She was so exquisitely beautiful, would that I had half of her beauty. The thought of Gareth caused my heart to skip a beat. His proposal in the morning room had been a gallant gesture, but he'd only done it to make things easier for me, once he'd rescued me from his ruthless brother and from Estelle also, but surely any man would have helped a lady in distress.

He'd altered the master bedroom, but with what thought in mind, to please me or to ensure that I would share his bed? I walked over to Lizzie's sampler on the wall. Gently running my hand over it, I made a silent plea, help me, Grandmother, show me what is right.

After some thought I decided to seek out Gareth for I needed to speak to him. As I walked down the staircase I looked over the banister and recalled the evening I witnessed Estelle's outburst.

I tried the dining-room first for he sometimes lingered over his port. As I opened the door I knew this wasn't going to be easy. Gareth was sitting alone at the table, a glass in his hand. He looked at me with some surprise.

'Why, Silvia, I thought that you had retired for the night. What ails you, for you look pale.' His voice held concern and for a brief moment I hesitated before I spoke.

'I'm sorry, Gareth. I cannot marry you. For now at least we must cancel our wedding.' With these words I left him. He looked stunned and as I climbed the staircase to my room, I heard him call my name.

'Silvia, an explanation is called for.'

But tonight I could not explain anything for I hardly knew the answer myself.

9

'I am mortified, Silvia,' my mother's voice berated me next morning when I was hardly awake. 'You have your dress and the church booked, what are you thinking about.' As she spoke, Mother paced up and down my room.

'It is not about gowns and churches, Mother,' I replied quietly.

'Then what is it about? Tell me for I am interested to know why you have called off your wedding to such a catch as Gareth.' Mother spoke harshly.

'Love Mother! It is about love!' I stressed the word.

'And what would you know of love at your tender age?' Mother scoffed.

'I know I feel love, but it is not returned. I cannot marry a man that does not love me, Mother.' I uttered with sincerity.

'Well, he'll certainly not love you now

and that's a fact.' She laughed as she spoke. 'And who's to pick up the pieces and cancel all the arrangements?'

'I shall do it myself today,' I offered. 'And it doesn't mean I'll never marry Gareth.'

'You can be sure he wouldn't consider marrying you after this charade,' Mother interrupted, waving one arm in the air as she spoke. I could see she was getting more agitated by the second.

'Calm down, Mother,' I pleaded.

'Calm down! When you've brought nothing but shame and disappointment upon me, and what will your Aunt Rachel think? Tell me that.' Her voice was getting louder.

'Aunt Rachel will understand.' As I spoke the words I was sure that this would be so.

'Understand!' exclaimed Mother. 'What I suggest, my girl, is that you come back with me today to Exeter, for that is where I shall be going as soon as it can be arranged.'

'I have no intention of leaving Darkwood,' I said stubbornly. 'For my intention is to get to know Gareth better.' Mother headed to the door, before opening it she indicated with her hand to the ivory gown still hanging on the picture rail.

'And what are you to do with this pray tell me, for it cost a pretty penny?'

'My intention is to store it in the wardrobe and wear it one day soon.' I hoped my voice held conviction. Mother tossed her head with an air of contempt and slammed the door behind her, while I stood on a chair and lifted down my wedding gown and laid it across the bed.

Sometime later Pru came to me, 'The mistress is in a foul mood, Silvia, and says that we are to go home today.' As she spoke, Pru dabbed a handkerchief at her eyes. I got up from the armchair and placed one arm around her shoulder.

'Please don't cry, Pru,' I entreated. 'You can stay with me if you care to, for

Kitty will look after Mother.'

'Could I really, Miss? Oh I'd like that.' Pru's face lit up and as quickly looked crestfallen again. 'But I'd need permission from your mother.'

'Don't worry,' I consoled, 'I'll speak to Mother on your behalf.' It was quite a battle, but Mother agreed to Pru staying with me understanding that I'd be left alone without a maid.

Mother left Darkwood with all her belongings at one o'clock that same afternoon, Aunt Rachel and I stood on the path waving until the carriage was out of sight. I felt a great sadness in my heart which Aunt Rachel must have sensed for she took my arm and suggested that we have a cup of tea in the drawing-room.

'Silvia,' began Aunt Rachel as she poured tea for the two of us. 'If you are not ready for marriage to Gareth I do understand, but may I ask how you feel about him?'

'I truly love him Aunt, but before I can marry him I need to know that he loves me too. I cannot condone marrying someone for the wrong reasons, for some time I thought I could, but realised last night it would be the wrong thing to do,' I replied truthfully.

'And you have no misgivings?' My aunt inquired.

'None at all,' I replied emphatically.

'This is all that matters. Now I want you to go and rest in your room and come down to dinner this evening looking your best for I shall ensure Gareth joins us. In the meantime, I shall call at the vicarage and explain to Mr Poulter and Isabel, I will also need to get a letter to our relations at Lydford.' How kind my aunt's words were, so different from Mother's and I wondered how two sisters could be so different.

'And what of Estelle?' I asked, suddenly thinking of her also.

'Estelle is indisposed and could be for some time, but I don't want you to worry your pretty little head about it.

Now run along and I'll see you at dinner.' My aunt's voice was firm and would brook no argument.

I sat in my room by the fire all afternoon mulling things over in my mind, and praying Gareth would not be adverse to joining us for dinner that evening, for I longed to see him. Pru carefully put my wedding gown away in the wardrobe covering it with muslin. That evening it took me some time to decide what to wear. I decided on the lemon-coloured silk with the scooped neckline, simply because I'd worn it on the first evening Gareth had addressed me by my christian name.

I asked Pru to fashion my hair the same as well, covering it as the back with the snood that matched my dress. I tried to recreate the effect of that previous evening which seemed so long ago. I clasped the cream pearls at my neck and slipped the ruby and diamond betrothal ring on my finger, it sparkled in the light of the lamp and I knew that to wear it would be a statement for Gareth, hopefully conveying the message that I was still betrothed to him.

Looking in the drawer of the dressing table for a handkerchief, I chanced on the lace bag belonging to Lizzie which I had placed here on the day of our arrival at Darkwood after finding it at the bottom of the wardrobe.

The yellow roses were almost the colour of the dress I wore, and thought to take it to dinner with me. I pressed the lace to my cheek feeling close to my beloved grandmother who I felt sure had guided me last night.

Putting the bag on the top of the dressing table I selected a pretty white lace handkerchief which I intended to place in the bag. Opening the twisted gold clasp I went to push the handkerchief inside when I felt something tucked in the bag, taking it out I could see that it was a folded envelope very like the ones in Lizzie's writing desk. I took it over to the armchair and sat down unfolding the envelope. I looked at it back and front several times.

Although it was sealed, I could see nothing had been written on it. I got up and went to the desk and took an envelope out, it matched perfectly to the one I'd found. Sitting back in the armchair I considered what to do.

Part of me said that I should take it to Aunt Rachel, but my heart said to open it as I'd found it. The lace bag had obviously been overlooked when the wardrobe had been cleared out. I looked again in the bag to see if it held anything else. Reaching my hand in the bottom I touched on a small metal object. On bringing it out into the light of the lamp I could see it was a small brass key, probably the one missing from the desk.

I'd discovered it too late as Douglas had put a new lock on only the other day, so I tucked the key back in the bag. Holding the envelope again for some time I made a decision, right or wrong to open it myself for she was my grandmother and I loved her. My hand was unsteady as I unsealed it, thinking that this had lain unseen for many years.

There was a sheet of paper inside which at first I was reluctant to remove. My heart pounding, I eventually found the courage to retrieve it, unfolding it I could see bold handwriting written in blue ink which had faded a little over the years. Tears stung my eyes as I saw the name Lizzie at the bottom of the page. I lay my hand which held the letter on my lap trying to pull myself together before reading something that had been written so long ago. It could be a letter never posted to her family or an invitation, things I'd mulled over before when the desk was first opened, but unless I read it I'd never know. Nothing could have prepared me for the content of the letter as I read.

April the 23rd 1851.

No longer can I stand Samuel's infidelity. I see Jared's face at every turn to remind me of it, my heart bleeds for his mother, Kate, who died giving birth to him at the tender age of sixteen years.

I lay no blame on her, she was just a child and would have succumbed to Samuel's persuasive ways with women as I surrendered to it long ago. I have some sympathy for Jared not knowing his true parentage, will he ever know that he is Samuel's illegitimate son? The sad fact is that after laying him at Rachel's door he disowned him, I feel I should lay bare to Jared the truth, but can no longer endure Samuel's wrath either, and now the servants are gossiping yet again that a girl in the village is with child by Samuel.

I cannot bear their hushed silence as I walk into a room or the glances of sympathy in my direction. Whoever reads this first will know why I must end my misery and explain it to my beloved grandchildren, Gareth and Silvia, when they are old enough *to understand it. Gareth who is full of endearing ways already and Silvia who at such a young age appreciates the written word.*

My heart is heavy that I shall not see them grow into adulthood, but my depression is such that I can no longer carry on. The laudanum awaits me, calling me and I have to reach for it, Samuel will despise me for it, that I would dare to escape in this way, but that is the trump card I shall forever hold over him for I have no other and I shall lie forever surrounded by the bluebells in Darklady's Wood.

Lizzie.

I could not at first take it in, Jared's name jumped up at me as I looked at the letter again, I could hardly believe it. Jared was Samuel's son, or should I believe it? And I recalled the cruel twist of his mouth and ruthless manner so like my grandfather, and that led me to think that Jared was in truth my uncle.

A sob escaped my lips as I realised my beloved Lizzie appeared to have taken her own life because of my grandfather's cruelty and philandering ways. Oh my Lord, I thought, clutching the letter to my bosom and recalling the words, *I shall lie forever surrounded by the bluebells in Darklady's Wood*. She had taken the laudanum in that beautiful wood and lay to die on a carpet of bluebells, I could not bear it, I needed someone to share this pain with me and my thoughts flew to Gareth, *my beloved grandchildren, Gareth and Silvia*.

I stood up tears streaming down my face, tucking the letter back into the lace bag intent on finding Gareth before dinner, was there no end to my misery? The thought ran through my mind, Gareth's endearing ways, was I so wrong to doubt him, wrong to tell him that I could not marry him on the foundation that he had not declared his love for me?

My feet practically ran along the

corridor, sobs escaping my lips as I ran, my hand tightly clutching the bag lest someone take it from me. The fact that I didn't know which was Gareth's room hadn't occurred to me. I ran blindly on, the skirts of my lovely dress dragging along the carpet as another miracle happened and Gareth stepped out of the master bedroom into the corridor.

'Gareth, Gareth!' I shouted, sobs still racking my body as I tumbled headlong into his arms, his arms went around me cradling my head on his shoulder, no matter how I tried I couldn't stop crying, I'd never felt such despair.

'Silvia, sshhh,' he whispered trying to calm me but to no avail so he led me into the bedroom which he'd so caringly refurbished for me, the thought of which made me worse. He sat me in the armchair by the fire which was still burning in the hearth and pulled a bell cord that I had not noticed before.

Leaning on the floor before me he tried so hard to pacify me, in no time at all Dotty appeared, her eyes were like saucers taking in the scene before her, we would be the talk of the kitchen, but I didn't care. My dishevelled hair, red cheeks and sobs would be relayed to the cook no doubt.

'Dotty, please fetch Miss Silvia a large brandy and tell no-one,' Gareth instructed the bewildered girl. 'Now Silvia please tell me what causes you such distress.'

'Jared . . . Jared . . . ' I sobbed looking Gareth in the eye, I must have looked a sight. 'Jared is not your brother, he is our uncle!' I paused for breath, 'And our beloved grandmother took her own life in Darklady's Wood! Oh Gareth, I cannot bear it.'

Dotty arrived with the brandy, Mrs Trigg at her heels.

'Is there something wrong, sir?' Knowing full well there was, as she took in the scene before her.

'Please leave us, Mrs Trigg and tell no-one,' said Gareth, thrusting the glass of brandy into my trembling hand.

'But the mistress is asking for you both, sir. What shall I tell her?' Mrs Trigg persisted.

'Tell them we'll be down soon, Mrs Trigg please, now leave us.'

'Come along, Dotty,' said Mrs Trigg pushing the girl through the door, taking her displeasure out on the poor child. I gulped the brandy, clutching the glass with a trembling hand, and thankfully the sobs subsided.

'I know you are distraught dear heart, but tell me how you found this out,' Gareth asked softly.

'I found this letter in Lizzie's bag.' And I fumbled to unclasp the bag and handed Gareth the letter, sobs starting again as I handled it. Gareth stood by the fireplace slowly reading the words which must have been as painful to him.

'This would explain why we can't find Lizzie's grave, for it would be in unconsecrated ground. I can understand your distress for I feel it to, but we need to tell my mother, for it would appear she could shed further light on all this.' Gareth spoke sensibly I realised and at last I was beginning to calm myself, sound sense was suddenly replacing hopelessness.

'You are right, Gareth, but I need to freshen up and do something with my hair,' I said to him and once again he rang the bell. On this occasion Mrs Trigg answered it.

'Yes, sir,' she said with a hint of dissatisfaction.

'Please bring Miss Silvia a jug of hot water and a face cloth.'

Mrs Trigg returned once more with Dotty who carried a jug of water which she tipped slowly into a china washbowl on a stand near the door.

'Dinner is ready, sir,' Mrs Trigg addressed Gareth as she spoke, 'What shall I tell your mother?'

'I shall come down and speak to her myself. Now that will be all, I thank both of you.' No sooner had Gareth spoken than the housekeeper and Dotty left the room.

'I cannot go down to dinner Gareth, for I could not eat a thing, this has upset me so much.' My voice was almost a whisper as I held the warm face cloth to my burning cheeks and eyes.

'Don't fret, I will go down to Mother and explain that you are feeling unwell, and that we will see her and Father in the drawing-room afterwards if you are able. I will fetch you a towel,' he said thoughtfully. When he handed it to me some seconds later he asked, 'Shall I send Pru to you to tidy your beautiful hair?'

'Yes please Gareth, you are so kind, however could I have thought . . . ' My voice trailed off, not wishing to tell him that I'd misconstrued his motive for marrying me. Another sob escaped my lips at the thought of it.

'Silvia, calm yourself.' As he spoke he laid his hands gently on my shoulders and planted a kiss on my cheek.

'Pru will need my hairbrush,' I said suddenly thinking logically. 'Maybe I should go back to my room.'

'No,' Gareth said emphatically. 'I wish you to stay here where I can keep an eye on you. I shan't be gone long, I promise.' As he left I felt bereft without his calming presence and wished with all my heart I could return to yesterday.

Pru arrived with a hairbrush not long after Gareth left, she'd also brought with her a powder puff. I sat at the dressing table on a soft brocade chair and looked at my reflection in the mirror while Pru brushed and re-arranged my hair.

'It's not for me to ask what troubles you, Miss Silvia, but what I do know is that the young gentlemen who is to be your husband is most concerned about you and that's a fact.' As she spoke Pru skilfully rearranged the snood and then set to dabbing my cheeks with the powder puff. When she'd finished I certainly looked better and somehow older and wiser for the experience of the past days. I wished so much to put right my relationship with Gareth, but knew that it would have to wait until other issues had been resolved.

An hour later, Gareth and I entered the drawing-room together, Aunt Rachel and Uncle William were on the settle together by the fire.

'What is amiss?' Aunt Rachel asked anxiously. As I looked at her I thought how much like her mother she looked, a fact I'd not noticed before. Aunt Rachel got up and walked towards me placing a protective arm around my shoulder and seated me on the matching settle opposite. Uncle William was by the fire. Although warm, the cold blue walls chilled me and I shuddered.

Gareth took a seat next to me. 'Where did you find that reticule?' Aunt Rachel exclaimed as she seated herself once more. 'I do believe it belonged to my mother.' As she spoke I could feel the tears pricking my eyes once more, my throat burned and I could not speak, but Gareth answered his mother.

'You are right, Mother, it is indeed Lizzie's lace bag. Silvia found it in the wardrobe the day of her arrival at Darkwood, but until today had not picked it up.' Gareth continued while my aunt looked at him as if spellbound. 'The cause of Silvia's distress is a letter she found in the bag, which has been written by your mother and reveals to us secrets which we had not known until now.'

Saying this Gareth took the bag gently from me, unclasped it and handed Lizzie's letter to Aunt Rachel. The room was silent except for the occasional crackling of a log on the fire as she read it, she then folded the letter and passed it back to Gareth.

'It is true, my children.' Aunt Rachel spoke in a hushed voice. 'Your grandmother did take the laudanum on that very day in the wood, your grandfather found her a couple of hours later lying under a tree among the bluebells. He never forgave her as she so rightly says, for escaping him that way, her lifeless body was carried back to the house by Douglas who was younger then.' Aunt

Rachel looked in some kind of trance as she continued. 'The lovely fur-trimmed green cloak she wore was removed and banished to the attic.'

'I saw it,' I interrupted, 'On the top of her clothes in a chest in the attic.' The thought of it causing tears to swim before my eyes.

'My father was adamant she would not be buried in the churchyard, but outside the boundary wall with no headstone to mark this beautiful lady's final resting place. But I have tended her grave all these years.' She stopped, her emotion overcoming her.

'And what of Jared who I have always thought of as my brother?' Gareth's questioning voice cut the silence.

'He is indeed my half-brother, Samuel's son. He so wanted a son and asked me to bring him up as my own so he could live at Darkwood. Jared turned out to be as cruel as his father and had no love for Samuel, so Jared was disowned from an early age.' Again my aunt stopped, obviously reliving the past which Lizzie's letter had brought to her mind.

'And where is Jared now?' My voice was strong once more, 'He needs to be told the truth of his parentage,' I insisted.

'We've not seen Jared since your banns of marriage were called on Sunday.' Uncle William spoke for the first time. I had quite forgotten he was there opposite me.

'And will you tell him, Aunt Rachel, when he reappears?' I asked quietly.

'Yes, I will, for as I say he needs to know the truth for many reasons,' she agreed.

'And my grandmother's portrait? Do you know who disfigured the likeness of her lovely face with such hatred?' I asked, keen to have all the mysteries surrounding Lizzie solved.

'I can answer that,' offered Uncle William. 'Your aunt does not know this for I spared her any more unhappiness. It was Samuel, I saw him as I walked along the corridor repeatedly slash at her face with inane fury. It was I who took the portrait down and with Douglas' help placed it in the attic so Rachel would not see it.'

Uncle William paused and then continued, 'Samuel then had his portrait painted in defiance of Lizzie's death, by a tree in Darklady's Wood, and he hung it deliberately at the top of the stairs where his wife's portrait had been.'

'Is there anything else you have to tell us?' Gareth spoke quietly looking from his father to his mother as he spoke.

'For my part at least,' said Uncle William leaning forward in his seat, 'The only thing I know is that Samuel instructed that the walls of the drawing-room and dining-room be painted the colour of the bluebells so no-one would forget what Lizzie did to him. His anger was so fierce he never forgave her.'

'And you, Mother? Have you any further revelations we should know about?' As Gareth spoke my aunt looked at both of us deliberating whether she should tell us more.'

'Estelle.' She spoke the name and it had hung in the air between us, almost tangible, and the sound of her name being spoken conjured up to me the sound of Estelle's beautiful melodic voice and laugh which I'd heard and loathed on the evening of my arrival at Darkwood.

'What of Estelle, for I already know that she is unsound of mind,' said Gareth as if breaking a spell which had been cast on us all.

'She is Samuel's illegitimate child too,' said Aunt Rachel, wiping a tear from her eye with the back of her hand. 'Such a beautiful child but her mother was deranged and died not long ago in a mental institution. I very much fear that Estelle will follow in her footsteps.'

At this point Aunt Rachel did cry. What secrets she had carried these past years and how difficult it must have been for her, and I knew now why she strived so hard to keep Estelle apart from Jared and Gareth, for she was

Jared's half-sister and Gareth's aunt.

Gareth and I left my aunt and uncle to spend much needed moments together. As we were leaving the room, Aunt Rachel looked up and said, 'I will show you both Lizzie's grave tomorrow.' We both nodded in agreement.

Gareth walked me back to my room dropping a kiss on my brow as he left me saying he would join me for breakfast. 'Sleep well dear heart,' he said.

As I climbed wearily into bed that night thoughts of Lizzie whirled in my head, but I was thankful the mystery was solved. Uppermost in my mind was the thought that I needed to tell Gareth the secret of my heart which was that I loved him so very much. With that thought, I drifted into a restless sleep, my dreams were of beautiful Estelle and I knew she would forever haunt me.

10

'You look so dark under the eyes, Miss,' said Pru the next day, 'And your eyelids are all puffed up.'

'Do I really look that bad?' I questioned with some dismay going across to have a look in the mirror. Looking closely I could see what she meant, but under the circumstances I could have looked far worse.

'I agree with you Pru, but nothing can be done about it,' I said with some resignation.

'What will you wear today?' Pru asked, and I went over to the window to see if there were blue or grey skies today. Pulling back the pink curtains I could see it was a glorious day, the sun shone in a cloudless blue sky and as far as I could tell there was hardly any breeze. I knew we were going to the graveyard today and recalled how cold it had been on the first day we had come to Darkwood.

As I looked from the window I could see primroses growing in the flower border and I thought to pick a bunch to lay on Lizzie's grave. Thinking of it I felt my throat ache and quickly went to the wardrobe to choose what I would wear. As I looked through my array of gowns I touched on my wedding gown, which caused me to think how I should have been marrying Gareth in two days' time.

I thought back to the day that Gareth had first seen me here in this very room. The memory helped me decide what to wear and I lifted out the pale blue dress I'd been wearing on my arrival that day. I then lifted down the blue bonnet which matched the gown, and handed it to Pru.

'I know why you've picked this, Miss,' she said, helping me into the silk dress, 'But it's not my place to make a comment and that's a fact.'

'You are right in your assumption,

Pru, and I am quite happy for you to say whatever is on your mind,' and added, 'for today at least.'

'Well Miss, if that's the case I'd just like to say I hope you and the young gentleman can put things right and very soon,' Pru bravely answered.

'And so do I, Pru,' I acknowledged adjusting the skirt of the dress and flattening the lace collar. 'I'll wear my cameo brooch today for Grandmother gave it to me when I admired it as a child.' At the words I had another fleeting thought about the events of yesterday and tried to dismiss it from my mind or I would start weeping again.

After Pru had arranged my hair, I went down to breakfast, for the first time Uncle William, Aunt Rachel and Gareth were sitting at the table, they all looked at me as I entered the room. I took a seat which Gareth held for me, quite the gentleman I thought. However could I have doubted his intentions, I so desperately needed to talk to him but needed to wait until we had visited the graveyard.

Little was said at the breakfast table other than Aunt Rachel asking, 'How are you today, Silvia?'

'I feel a little better thank you, Aunt,' I responded quietly. It was true in as much as I wasn't spilling tears everywhere, but inside I felt as if I had a huge knot in my stomach.

I'd fetched my bonnet and Pru had laid the cream shawl around my shoulders. 'Just in case you feel cold,' she had explained. The shawl caused me to think of Gareth and the bluebell wood. More unpleasant thoughts and question came into my head. Where is Jared?

We stepped into the April sunshine and I could see a very handsome landau with the roof folded back had been brought to the front of the house. Aunt Rachel and Uncle William seated themselves inside and Gareth indicated for me to do the same.

'One moment, Gareth please, I wish

to pick some flowers for our grandmother,' I explained.

'I'll come with you,' he said, following me to the flower border. The primroses were turning their pretty yellow heads to the sun and I felt almost cruel as I picked about twenty and arranged them in a small bunch which I asked Gareth to hold while I tied them with some pink ribbon I had found in my work basket.

'Silvia,' Gareth caught my arm gently as I was about to walk back to the carriage, his deep brown eyes looked at me appealingly, 'when we return to the house I need to speak with you alone,' he confessed.

'We are of the same mind, cousin,' I said with some relief, for he had saved me from broaching the subject myself which could have appeared quite unladylike.

Comfortably sitting in the carriage next to Gareth for all of our journey, I could see Culmoor Church perched on top of the hillock. My thoughts were in disarray, Lizzie, Gareth, Jared, Estelle and my wedding gown were all jumbled up in my head, and as hard as I tried I could not separate one from the other. We stopped near the graveyard as in that first day and my thought was that I had come around in a full circle in just over three weeks. The difference being that today instead of an icy wind a cool breeze blew pleasantly across my face.

Gareth by my side, we entered the graveyard following Aunt Rachel, with me clutching the posy I had picked for Lizzie. We walked among the gravestones to the far side and I could see Aunt Rachel unlatch a gate in the corner which I hadn't realised was there. We followed her through it and she led us behind the wall where halfway along I could see a mound of earth.

Thankfully the sun shone through the trees on to the grave which made me feel a little more at ease. I loathed to think of my grandmother lying in the cold earth away from the sunlight.

Gareth gently squeezed my arm to give me comfort. I noticed a small varnished wooden cross had been placed in the earth at one end, as I bent to look at it I could see the name, Elizabeth, had been lovingly carved into the wood with the date 1851.

I looked at Aunt Rachel. 'Now Grandfather is gone and has no bearing on this grave anymore we should place a small headstone here, Aunt.' I'd made a statement which I felt very strongly about, for this lovely lady who was my grandmother, had taken her life because of a grandfather who caused her nothing but pain.

'I agree with Silvia,' Gareth spoke up. 'The wooden cross is admirable but not enough.'

'We will order one,' agreed Aunt Rachel. 'We should get back for I feel all of us have endured enough,' she said quietly.

'Could you please leave me here a moment?' I asked tentatively, 'For there is something I wish to say to Grandmother alone.'

'But of course, dear,' said Aunt Rachel placing a cold hand over mine. She suddenly seemed more her normal self, perhaps bringing us here had been a trial for her, and now the deed was accomplished she felt more at ease. I stood amongst the trees, bending down I laid the posy of primroses on the sandy coloured earth.

'I found you,' I whispered, 'and would never have stopped searching, I love you and Gareth also, please lead me on the right path with him and help me choose my words wisely.' So saying I walked back to the carriage feeling a great sense of peace. Gareth was waiting to assist me as I climbed in and all the way back to Darkwood his hand lay closed over mine.

Stepping on to the path outside the house Gareth detained me while his mother and father walked on inside.

'It is time for us now, Silvia. For there is something I want to say to you,'

Gareth's words conveyed to me that he was as eager to say what was on his mind, as was I. We agreed to talk in the morning-room and, as we stepped through the door of this delightful room, I cast my mind back to the last time we were here together when Gareth had proposed to me and slipped the betrothal ring on my finger.

As if reading my thoughts Gareth said, 'You are not wearing the ring today.' As he spoke I removed my bonnet and lay it on the table by the door.

'Only because I feared I may lose it,' I answered as I sat in the armchair while Gareth turned his mother's chair around to sit on.

'Silvia, I don't know why you said you wouldn't marry me, but before you say anything, I'd like to explain myself if I may,' he said questioningly.

'Please do, Gareth, for I ardently wish to know your thoughts,' I replied, impatience welling up inside me.

'When our grandfather's Will was

read and I came to your room I was determined to dislike you, but at the same time determined to marry you for the sake of this house.' He paused momentarily, standing up, arms behind his back, he started pacing the floor. 'And then I admired you for your liking of Tennyson and Dickens, what I hadn't expected was to fall in love with you.'

'Oh Gareth,' I exclaimed, 'if only you had declared this before I cancelled our wedding, I was so sure you didn't love me.'

'And do you love me?' he asked, stopping his pacing he stood before me.

'Without hesitation I can say yes, I do love you,' I declared.

'And will you marry me?' he asked, raising one dark eyebrow in question.

'Yes Gareth, I will marry you,' I agreed, breathing a sigh of relief that this conversation had gone well. He took my hand and pulling me to my feet drew me near to him.

'Then let us marry on Saturday as arranged.' The words he spoke made my heart sing and I was happy once more.

'But the church is cancelled,' I said with some alarm.

'We can rebook it, the banns have been called.' The words made me think of Estelle. 'Now what has distressed you, darling?'

'It is nothing,' I answered untruthfully.

'I can tell by your face it is something.' Gareth's words showed how astute he had become at assessing my emotions. 'Now tell me for we must have no secrets between us.'

'It is Estelle.' My voice faltered. 'What will become of her, Gareth? For she is so lovely.'

'Dear heart, Estelle is being cared for by the nuns at an Abbey not far from here, it is for the best. My mother arranged it. Now smile for me please and tell me that you are happy,' he coaxed.

'Now let us go and tell my father and mother,' suggested my husband-to-be, dropping a gentle kiss on my lips, nothing felt matter of fact or unemotional now.

Uncle William and Aunt Rachel were delighted. While Gareth went to Culmoor to the vicarage with Uncle William, I stayed to talk with my aunt.

'So Silvia, you are now ready for marriage to my son?' she asked seriously.

'Completely and without doubt, Aunt, for I know the union is for love. It is such a pity Mother is not here, and what of Jared?' I asked, anxious to know what had become of him.

'It is a shame about your mother. She left far too hastily and as for Jared, he'll turn up one day like the prodigal son.' This led me to believe that my aunt had experienced this problem before with the ruthless son of the ruthless Samuel.

'Aunt Rachel,' I said cautiously, 'there is one thing about your mother I wish so much to know.'

'Ask me child, for it will not distress me now,' said my aunt.

'Whereabouts in the wood was Lizzie found?' The question had been burning in my mind since we had left the graveyard.

'I can show you if it will not cause you any more pain.' My aunt looked at me gently as she spoke.

'I'd like that, it will lay the ghost to rest completely,' I answered truthfully.

Aunt Rachel and I walked together in the sunshine across the bridge, stopping for some seconds to watch the river sparkling in the sun. As we neared the wood both of us looked at each other.

'It is so beautiful Silvia, a carpet of blue, I can see why my mother loved it here.' As she spoke we stepped on the path between the bluebells, as I followed Aunt Rachel I knew that we were following Lizzie's last steps.

Passing the tree that Jared had pushed me against, I thought of that moment and how Gareth had stepped in to save me. We walked farther into the wood until I could see we were nearly at the other side.

Just as we were about to step into the sunshine, Aunt Rachel stopped and indicated the tree where Samuel had his portrait painted. I felt anger, anger at a man who could be so cruel as to stand where his loving wife had died and then have the audacity to hang the picture at the top of the staircase for everyone to see.

How I hated him and all he stood for and I vowed then that when I was Mistress of Darkwood in two days' time that I would have the portrait burned and the blue walls painted in the green and pink my grandmother had loved. I would thwart him as Lizzie had, and with that thought in my mind I walked back through the bluebell wood with a strength I never had before.

* * *

The morning of my wedding day dawned and I hardly dared draw back the curtains, but when I did I could see that the sun shone for us in a cloudless sky. We were to be married at twelve o'clock. Before getting ready, Aunt Rachel asked me to go to the dining-room and on stepping inside I was astounded to see that, as if by magic, the walls had been painted a pale green overnight.

The wedding breakfast was laid, the table looked so inviting with an ivory cloth covering it on which had been laid silver knives, forks, spoons and serviette holders also pretty rose-coloured dishes and in the centre of it all was a beautifully-decorated two-tier wedding cake.

'Aunt Rachel, thank you so much,' I said kissing her on the cheek.

'It is my pleasure, and here is a small gift from me to remember your wedding day by.' As she spoke my aunt offered me a small oblong package. On removing the tissue paper I could see with delight it was a lovely handstitched book mark with Gareth's name and mine in green and the date of our marriage the 15th of April 1865 in gold, underneath were the words, *God bless you both*.

'I shall treasure it,' was all I could say, for I suddenly felt an emotion, not sad but happy and I could have twirled Aunt Rachel round the dining-room, but a sense of decorum prevented me from doing so.

As we stepped back into the hall a familiar voice boomed out, 'So Silvia, you've changed your mind again, most inconvenient as I was just getting settled, now here we are again.' Before I turned in the direction of the voice I knew it was Mother, it could be no-one else, she had a bit of Samuel in her, not cruel but domineering.

'Mother!' I exclaimed and I thought my happiness would never end.

'Come on, child, I need a hand or I'll never be ready.' As she spoke Aunt Rachel and I threw back our heads and laughed. 'This is a solemn occasion Silvia and I'll thank you to remember that, and you Rachel,' Mother admonished with a rare smile on her face.

Isabel arrived full of excitement and Pru could hardly contain herself, not helping at all really just bustling about, my only hope was that she could keep still long enough to do my hair. Just before we got ready there was a tap at the door, it was Gareth.

'You can't come in, sir!' shrieked Pru, 'it's bad luck.'

'If you could just hand this to the bride and tell her it's to match her eyes.'

I could hear Gareth's deep voice, 'And this is for her bridesmaid. Tell the lovely Silvia, I'll see her at the altar.' Pru shut the door swiftly and turned to us.

'Oh look, Miss,' she said and broke into tears, 'it's so lovely, it really is so lovely.' I looked at what Gareth had handed to Pru, for me a posy of violets wrapped in lace with an ivory silk ribbon and for Isabel a posy of white primulas also wrapped in lace with a blue ribbon.

We stood ready Isabel and I,

complimenting each other on how we looked, as we glanced in the mirror the reflection looking back at us appeared so different from the other day in as much that it really looked like me, the lace veil was exquisite and I could see my black hair shining through it.

I looked down at my feet and the dainty half-boots of silk, and said to myself, 'Enjoy this day for you will never look or feel like this again.'

Mother wore a light purple gown with a matching bonnet and I noticed she carried a white lace handkerchief. Aunt Rachel wore a dress of pale rose-coloured silk with a rose pink bonnet, Pru had been told she could attend the service and wore her best outfit, a pale green dress, her mop of red hair escaping a matching green bonnet.

As Isabel and I walked down the staircase my thought was that when I walked up it next time I would be Mrs Hunter.

I clung to Uncle William's arm as we

walked up to the church gate, Isabel close behind us also I suspected savouring every moment, she did indeed look like a brightly coloured butterfly, the moth had disappeared and I intended it to stay that way.

As I walked down the aisle on Uncle William's arm to meet my bridegroom, the sun's rays slanted through the windows and every few steps we were caught in a beam of light which momentarily obscured my vision. But as I reached Gareth's side my heart skipped a beat for he looked more handsome than ever, his coal black hair and dark eyes shining, dressed in a black jacket, trousers and waistcoat with a white ruffled shirt that suited him perfectly and I notice through a haze of sudden brief tears that he wore a violet in his lapel. As he looked at me and smiled he whispered, 'You look captivating.' And then I heard George Poulter's voice.

'Dearly beloved, we are gathered . . . ' And I knew today there would be no interruption.

We stepped out as man and wife, rice was thrown and a voice held our attention for a moment.

'Good luck, brother.' It was Jared, I looked at him and thought of what he needed to be told, but not today and I felt some compassion for him in spite of the incident in the bluebell wood.

Much later I said to Gareth, 'I desire to walk with you in the fresh air, husband.' He smiled an engaging smile.

'Whatever my beautiful wife wishes,' he replied. So we walked to the bridge, it was a warm night and as we stood there together I looked back at the house, moonlight bathed the walls and I knew Darkwood was at peace having relinquished its secrets.

I turned back to Gareth, 'I have something for you.' And out of his pocket he took a small book, on looking at it closely I could see it was a red leather bound volume of Tennyson's *Lady Of Shallot*.

I was lost for words, but not my

husband, 'For when the moon was overhead, came two young lovers lately wed,' so saying he took me in his arms, I looked at the window of the master bedroom and thought with some joy that tonight I would share it with my husband whom I loved with all my heart, and reaching up to him our lips met in a slow lingering kiss and I knew Grandmother would have approved of our love for each other. We drew apart and walked back to Darkwood to start our lives together for always.

THE END

We do hope that you have enjoyed reading this large print book.

Did you know that all of our titles are available for purchase?

We publish a wide range of high quality large print books including:
Romances, Mysteries, Classics
General Fiction
Non Fiction and Westerns

Special interest titles available in large print are:
The Little Oxford Dictionary
Music Book, Song Book
Hymn Book, Service Book

Also available from us courtesy of Oxford University Press:
Young Readers' Dictionary
(large print edition)
Young Readers' Thesaurus
(large print edition)

For further information or a free brochure, please contact us at:

Other titles in the
Linford Romance Library:

THE FOOLISH HEART

Patricia Robins

Mary Bradbourne's aunt brought her up after her parents died. When she was ten, her aunt had a son, Jackie, who was left with a mental disability as the result of an accident. Unselfish and affectionate, Mary dedicated her life to caring for him. But when she meets Dr. Paul Deal and falls in love with him she faces a dilemma. How will she be able to care for her cousin, when she knows she must follow her heart?

HEIRS TO LOVING

Rachel Ford

When Jenni Green went to trace her father's family in Brittany, she didn't know that she would keep running into Raoul Kerouac, known to everyone in the area as 'Monsieur Raoul'. Autocratically he organises a job for her in the local campsite, and pushes the *gendarmerie* to find Jenni's stolen handbag. Luckily they find it; unluckily Raoul sees it first — for the documents show that Jenni's real name is Eugénie Aimée Kerouac, part owner of the estate . . .

PETTICOAT PRESS

Sheila Lewis

It's 1901, and Eleanor Paton has ambitions to become a journalist, so she is devastated when her father appoints Stephen Walsh as the new editor to his newspaper. Stephen refuses to print her articles. Eleanor is determined to succeed, but a dangerous connection with a militant suffragette causes errors of judgement in her work. However, as her talent begins to flourish under Stephen's guidance, a family crisis threatens to part them forever — just when they have fallen in love.

LOVE'S GAMBLE

Louise Armstrong

When Sarah Gannon's papa gambles away the family home, she is forced to open a herbalist's shop to survive. The Duke of Whitewell, in gratitude for Sarah's visits and medicines, leaves her a generous legacy upon his death. However, the new Duke suspects the worst of their innocent relationship, and Sarah is scathing in return. With such rancour between them, she never suspects why winning back Tewit Manor hasn't made her happy. When will she realise that home is where the heart is?